**Welcome to the world
of Sydney Harbour Hospital**
**(or *SHH*… for short—
because secrets never stay hidden for long!)**

Looking out over cosmopolitan Sydney Harbour, Australia's premier teaching hospital is a hive of round-the-clock activity—with a *very* active hospital grapevine.

With the most renowned (and gorgeous!) doctors in Sydney working side by side, professional and sensual tensions run sky-high—there's *always* plenty of romantic rumours to gossip about…

Who's been kissing who in the on-call room? What's going on between legendary heart surgeon Finn Kennedy and tough-talking A&E doctor Evie Lockheart? And what's wrong with Finn?

Find out in this enthralling new eight-book continuity from Mills & Boon® Medical™ Romance—indulge yourself with eight helpings of romance, emotion and gripping medical drama!

Sydney
From saving

Dear Reader

I'm not surprised that Sydney, one of the world's most beautiful cities, was chosen as the host city for a series of books, and I've loved writing book number four of the *Sydney Harbour Hospital* series. It's been especially fun as my husband's been working in Sydney recently, and I got to have a few weekend trips to the 'Emerald City'.

Being a tourist in a city is very different from being a resident, and that got me thinking about my hero, Tom Jordan. He's been away from Sydney for two years, and he's coming back to live in the same apartment and work at the same hospital. One random event has changed his life for ever and he's on a fast learning curve. Nothing in Sydney is the same, but one thing that hasn't changed is his belief that he doesn't need anybody's pity or help.

Hayley Grey is one exam away from being a qualified surgeon, and all her energies are consumed by work. She's spent years keeping busy so she doesn't have time to think about anything else, but a person can only run from something for so long before it catches up and starts to cause problems.

Ask Tom or Hayley if they're happy and they'll probably answer, 'I do all right.' Neither of them is prepared for what happens when they meet, and both of them are running scared.

I hope you enjoy their story as they slowly learn that to open one's heart and invite people in is the most valuable of life's lessons.

I love hearing from readers, and you can find me at www.fionalowe.com, harlequin.com, Facebook and Twitter.

Happy Reading!

Fiona

SYDNEY HARBOUR HOSPITAL: HOSPITAL: TOM'S REDEMPTION

BY
FIONA LOWE

First published in Great Britain 2012
by Mills & Boon, an imprint of Harlequin (UK) Limited.
Harlequin (UK) Limited, Eton House,
18-24 Paradise Road, Richmond, Surrey TW9 1SR

© Harlequin Books S.A. 2012

Special thanks and acknowledgement are given to Fiona Lowe
for her contribution to the *Sydney Harbour Hospital* series

ISBN: 978 0 263 89166 9

Harlequin (UK) policy is to use papers that are natural, renewable and recyclable products and made from wood grown in sustainable forests. The logging and manufacturing process conform to the legal environmental regulations of the country of origin.

Printed and bound in Spain
by Blackprint CPI, Barcelona

Always an avid reader, **Fiona Lowe** decided to combine her love of romance with her interest in all things medical, so writing Mills & Boon® Medical™ Romance was an obvious choice! She lives in a seaside town in southern Australia, where she juggles writing, reading, working and raising two gorgeous sons with the support of her own real-life hero!

Recent books by the same author:

CAREER GIRL IN THE COUNTRY
SINGLE DAD'S TRIPLE TROUBLE
THE MOST MAGICAL GIFT OF ALL
HER BROODING ITALIAN SURGEON
MIRACLE: TWIN BABIES

**These books are also available in eBook format
from www.millsandboon.co.uk**

*With special thanks to Leonie and Steve:
two terrific doctors
who generously shared their medical knowledge.*

Sydney Harbour Hospital

Sexy surgeons, dedicated doctors,
scandalous secrets, on-call dramas...

Welcome to the world of Sydney Harbour Hospital
(or *SHH*... for short—because secrets never stay hidden for long!)

In February new nurse Lily got caught up in the hotbed of hospital
gossip in **SYDNEY HARBOUR HOSPITAL: LILY'S SCANDAL**
by Marion Lennox

Then gorgeous paediatrician Teo
came to single mum Zoe's rescue in
SYDNEY HARBOUR HOSPITAL: ZOE'S BABY
by Alison Roberts

Last month sexy Sicilian playboy Luca finally met his match
SYDNEY HARBOUR HOSPITAL: LUCA'S BAD GIRL
by Amy Andrews

This month Hayley opens Tom's eyes to love in
SYDNEY HARBOUR HOSPITAL: TOM'S REDEMPTION
by Fiona Lowe

Join heiress Lexi as she learns to put the past behind her in May:
SYDNEY HARBOUR HOSPITAL: LEXI'S SECRET
by Melanie Milburne

In June adventurer Charlie helps shy Bella fulfil her dreams—
and find love on the way!
SYDNEY HARBOUR HOSPITAL: BELLA'S WISHLIST
by Emily Forbes

Then single mum Emily gives no-strings-attached surgeon Marco
a reason to stay in July
SYDNEY HARBOUR HOSPITAL: MARCO'S TEMPTATION
by Fiona McArthur

And finally join us in August as Ava and James
realise their marriage really is worth saving in
SYDNEY HARBOUR HOSPITAL: AVA'S RE-AWAKENING
by Carol Marinelli

And not forgetting *Sydney Harbour Hospital's* legendary heart surgeon
Finn Kennedy. This brooding maverick keeps his women on hospital
rotation... But can new doc Evie Lockheart unlock the secrets to his
guarded heart? Find out in this enthralling new eight-book continuity
from Mills & Boon® Medical™ Romance.

A collection impossible to resist!

These books are also available in ebook format
from www.millsandboon.co.uk

CHAPTER ONE

TOM JORDAN—Mr Jordan to almost everyone—stood on the balcony of his top-floor penthouse apartment with the winter sunshine warming his face. The harsh cry of seagulls wheeling above him clashed with the low and rumbling blast of a ferry's horn as the tang of salt hit his nostrils. All of it was quintessentially Sydney. The emerald city. *Home*.

He gazed straight ahead towards the Opera House with its striking sails and architectural splendour, before turning his head toward the iconic bridge on his right. He knew the scene intimately, having grown up in Sydney, although a *very* long way from this multimillion-dollar vantage point. As a kid he'd once taken the ferry to Taronga Park Zoo on a school excursion and been awed by the size of the mansions that clung to the shoreline for the breathtaking views. The teacher in charge had noticed him staring and had said, 'Dream on, Jordan. People like you only ever clean their floors.'

Tom had never forgotten that hard-nosed teacher or his words, which had eventually driven him to prove that teacher wrong. Prove everyone in Derrybrook wrong—well, almost everyone. Two people hadn't needed convincing because they'd always believed in him.

The penthouse and the Ferrari were his way of giving

those bastards from Derrybrook 'the finger'. The long, hard journey to being head of the world-renowned neurosurgery department at Sydney Harbour Hospital was another beast entirely—a personal tribute to one of life's special men.

His nostrils twitched as a slight musty aroma mixed in with the sharp citrus of cleaning products, drifted out from inside and lingered on the afternoon air. His cleaning lady had been both liberal and vigorous with their use in meeting the challenge of ridding the apartment of stale air—the legacy of having been closed up for well over a year. A year that had started out like any other, on a day that had been so routine it would have gone unnoticed in the annals of history yet for one tiny moment of mistiming, which had changed everything. Irrevocably. Irreversibly and indelibly.

For twenty-two months he'd stayed away from Sydney, not ever imagining he could return to the *one* place that represented everything he'd lost, but, just like that one moment in time, things had once again changed. Two months ago on Cottlesloe beach in Perth, the wind had whipped up in him an urge so strong it had had him contemplating heading east, but to what? A week later he'd received a joint invitation from Eric Frobisher, Medical Director of SHH, and Richard Hewitson, Dean of Parkes University's School of Medicine, inviting him to give a series of guest lectures over six weeks for staff and medical students. His initial reaction had been to refuse. He wasn't a teacher and lecturing wasn't what he wanted—it didn't even come close, but on a scale of necessity it was better than doing nothing at all. Doing nothing had sent him spiralling into a black hole that had threatened to keep him captive.

He gripped the balcony rails so tightly that the skin on

his knuckles burned. This past year had been all about 're-education' and was the first step onto the ladder of his new life. Once before he'd dragged himself up by the bootstraps and, by hell, he could do it again. He *had* to do it again. Only this time, unlike in his childhood, at least he wouldn't see their pity or disdain.

A nip in the air bit into him, making him shiver, and he turned slowly, reaching out his hands to feel the outdoor table. Having made contact, he counted five steps and commenced walking straight until his extended left hand pressed against the slightly open glass door. Running the fingers of his right hand down the pane, he kept them moving until they touched and then gripped the rectangular handle. He pulled the door fully open and stepped inside, barely noticing the change in light.

'And we're done. Good work, everyone. Thank you.' Hayley Grey, final-year surgical registrar, stepped back from the operating table and stripped off her gloves, leaving her patient in the capable hands of the anaesthetist and nursing staff. The surgery would later be described in the report as a routine appendectomy and only she and her night-duty team would know how close it had come to being a full-on disaster of septic shock with a peritoneum full of pus. Kylie Jefferson was an extremely lucky young woman. Another hour and things could have been very different.

Hayley pushed open the theatre swing doors, crossed the now quiet scrub-in area and exited through another set of doors until she was out in the long theatre suite corridor. She rolled back her shoulders as three a.m. fatigue hit her, taunting her with the luxury of sleep. Glorious and tempting sleep, which, she knew, if she gave in to and snuggled down in her bed, would only slap her hard and instantly depart with a bitter laugh. No, after years of experience she knew better than to try. She'd stick to her routine—type up her report on the computer, have something to eat, do an early round—and only then, as dawn was breaking, would she head home.

'Hayley, we've got cake.'

'What sort of cake?'

Jenny, the night-duty theatre nurse manager, rolled her eyes as Hayley walked into an unexpectedly busy staff lounge. Earlier in the night a road trauma case had put everyone on edge and Hayley had seen the tension on their faces when she'd arrived for her case. Two hours later, with the RT patient in ICU, the adrenaline had drained away, and the nursing staff was debriefing in the low-lit room, curled up on the couches and tucked up in warm theatre towels.

She automatically switched on the main bank of lights to make the room reassuringly brighter.

Hands flew to eyes as a chorus of 'It's too bright. Turn them off', deafened her.

Jenny compromised by turning off the set over the couches. 'After a month here, do you really have to ask what type of cake?'

Hayley gave a quiet smile. 'In that case I'll have the mud cake. Lucky I like chocolate.'

Although she'd only been at 'The Harbour' for four weeks, she'd already learned that the night-duty theatre team had an addiction to chocolate and caffeine, which, given their unsociable hours and the types of cases they often dealt with, was completely understandable. They were also an outgoing crew and although Hayley appreciated their friendliness, she often found it a bit daunting. Once she'd had a sister who had been as close a friend as a girl could ever have and, try as she might, she'd never been able to find the same sort of bond with anyone else. Sure, she had friends, but she always felt slightly disconnected. However, she could feel The Harbour staff slowly drawing her in.

'Everyone loves chocolate.' Jenny plated a generous triangle of the rich cake and passed it over.

'Tom Jordan didn't.' Becca, one of the scrub nurses, cradled her mug of coffee in both hands.

An audible sigh rolled around the room—one that combined the bliss of an en masse crush along with regret. This happened every single time someone mentioned the previous head of neurosurgery. Hayley had never met the man, but apparently he'd left the hospital without warning almost two years ago.

Hayley forked off some cake as she sat down. 'Is a man who doesn't like chocolate worth missing?'

'Hayley! You know not of what you speak.' Becca pressed her mug to her heart. 'Our Tom was divine. Sure, he took no prisoners, was known to reduce the occasional obtuse medical and nursing student to tears, but he never demanded more of you than he demanded of himself.'

'Which was huge, by the way,' added Theo, the only male nurse on the team. 'The man lived and worked here, and patients came ahead of everything and everyone. Still, I learned more from him than any other surgeon I've worked with.'

'Watching Tom operate,' Jenny gave a wistful smile, 'watching the magic he wove with those long fingers of his, you forgave him any gruff words he might have uttered during tense moments. One look from those sea-green eyes and we'd lay down our lives for him.'

'Suzy lay down with him,' Theo teased the nurse sitting next to him. 'But he got away. Who's your man of the moment? Rumour is it's Finn Kennedy.'

Suzy punched Theo hard on the arm. 'At least I experienced him once. You're just jealous.'

'Of Finn Kennedy? Not likely.' But the muscles around Theo's mouth had tightened.

Suzy shot Hayley a cool look. 'Theo quite fancied Tom, and the fact he's an amazing lover just makes Theo even sadder that he doesn't bat for his team.'

Hayley was used to the nurses teasing, but this time it all seemed way over the top. Laughing, she said, 'Gorgeous, talented, dedicated and a lover beyond Valentino? Now I *know* you're making this up.'

The aura of the room changed instantly and Jenny shot her a reproving look. 'No one could make Tom up. He's one of a kind.'

Hayley let the chocolate float on her tongue before swallowing another bite of the delicious cake. 'If he's so amazing and at the top of his game, why did he leave the prestigious Harbour?'

Becca grimaced. 'That's what we don't know. Tom took leave and then, without warning, management announced that Rupert Davidson would be acting head of Neuro while they searched the world for a new head. Then they clammed up when we asked questions.'

Jenny nodded. 'We've phoned Tom, but his number's no longer in use, we've done online searches, wondering if he took a job in the States or the UK, but the last entry about him was his final operation here. The man's gone to ground and doesn't want to be found.'

'I just hope that, wherever he is, he's working. Talent like that shouldn't be wasted.' Theo rose as the PA called the team into action. 'Oh, and, Hayley, we're competing against ICU to win the "Planet Savers" competition.

You're our weak link. Can you *please* turn off the lights when you leave?'

She bit her lip. 'I'll try.'

Having checked on her appendectomy patient, who was stable and sleeping, Hayley was now in the lift and on her way home. She leaned against the support rail and gave a blissful sigh. She loved this time of the night when dawn was close, but the hustle and bustle of the day was yet to start. It was a quiet and peaceful time—not always, but today all was calm and experience had taught her to savour the moment. The ping of the lift sounded and she pushed herself off the rail as the silver-coloured doors opened into the long, long corridor that connected the hospital with the basement staff car park. Sensor lights had been installed as part of the hospital's environmental policy, especially down here where, after the morning and evening's arrival and departure rush, the corridor was rarely used.

As she stepped out of the lift, she commenced counting in her head, expecting the lights to come on halfway between numbers one and two. She got to three and was now standing in the corridor, but there was still no greeting light. Not a single flicker. The lift doors closed behind her with a soft thud, stealing the only light, and inky, black darkness enveloped her. A shiver raced from head to toe, raising a trail of anxious goose bumps and her heart raced.

Just breathe.

Fumbling in her pocket, her fingers clamped around her phone. The lights had failed two nights ago and in a panic she'd rung Maintenance. Gerry had arrived in his overalls, taken one look at her terror-stricken face and had said, 'We've been having a bit of trouble with the sensor, but we've got a new one on order. If it ever happens again, love, you just do this,' and he'd quietly shown her where the override switch was located.

Why didn't I just walk to work?

Because it was dark. Come on, you know what to do.

She pressed a button on her phone and a tiny pool of light lit up her feet as she edged her way along the wall. Sweat dripped down her neck as the darkness pressed down on her, making it hard to move air in and out of her lungs. She thought she heard a sound and she stopped dead. Straining her ears to hear it again, she didn't move a muscle, but the moment passed and all she could hear was the pounding of her heart. She started moving again and stopped. This time she was sure she'd heard a *click-click* sound.

It's the bowels of the hospital. There are all sorts of noises down here. Just keep walking.

She wished she'd counted steps with Gerry last week, but she'd stuck to him like glue, listening only to his re-assuring voice. She continued edging along the wall until she felt the turn of the corridor pressing into her back. *You're halfway.* Knowing she was closer was enough to speed up her feet.

Click. Click. Tap. Tap. Tap. The sounds echoed around her like the boom of a cannon.

Her feet froze. Her breath stalled. *It's probably the furnace. Or pipes.*

God, she hated this. She was one exam away from being a fully qualified surgeon. She duelled with death on behalf of her patients every single day, winning more often than not. Facing down blood, guts and gore didn't faze her at all so she absolutely loathed it that the dark could render her mute and terrified.

You're close to the lights. Keep going.

Ten, nine, eight, seven... She silently counted backwards in her head as she scuttled sideways like a crab. Finally, she felt the bank of switches digging sharply into her spine. *Yes!* She swung around, pushed her eight fingers against the plastic and started pressing switches.

Bright, white light flickered and then filled the space with wondrously welcome light and Hayley rested her forehead against the cool wall in relief. She gulped in a couple of steadying breaths and just as her pulse stared to slow, she heard a click. She swung around and her scream echoed back to her.

'Are you hurt?' A tall man in black jeans, a black merino sweater and a black moleskin jacket turned from three metres away, holding something in his hand that she couldn't quite make out.

Her heart jumped in her chest and then pounded even harder, making her head spin, but somewhere buried in her fear a shot of indignation surged. 'No, I'm not bloody hurt, but you scared the living daylights out of me.'

'Why?' The question sounded surprised and he stared at her, but he didn't move to close the gap between them.

She threw her arms out as if the answer was self-evident. 'I didn't know you were here!'

His mouth twitched, but she didn't know if it was the start of a smile or the extension of a grimace. 'I've known you were here for the past few minutes.'

She blinked. 'How? It was pitch-black until a moment ago.'

His broad shoulders rose slightly and his empty hand flexed by his side. 'I heard the ping of the lift.'

'But that's in the other corridor and I might have gone in the opposite direction.'

'True, but you didn't. I could also smell you.'

Her mouth fell open at the matter-of-fact words and she

couldn't stop herself from raising one shoulder as she took a quick sniff of her armpit before looking back at him. His gaze hadn't shifted and offence poured through her. 'It's been a long night saving lives so sue me if I don't smell squeaky clean and fresh.'

'I didn't say it was offensive.'

Something about the way the deep timbre of his voice caressed the words should have reassured her and made her smile, but the fact he was still staring at her was utterly disconcerting. He hadn't made any move towards her, for which she was grateful, even though she could see a hospital ID lanyard hanging out of his pocket. With his black clothes, black hair, bladed cheekbones, a slightly crooked nose and a delicious cleft in his stubble-covered chin, he cut a striking image against the white of the walls. Striking and slightly unnerving. He wasn't a fatherly figure like Gerry the maintenance man in his overalls, neither did he have the easygoing manner of Theo. Neither of those men ever put her on edge.

Even so, despite her thread of anxiety, she would have had to be blind not to recognise he was handsome in a rugged, rough-edged kind of a way, and that was part of her unease. She had the feeling that his clothes were just a veneer of gentrification. Remove them and a raw energy would be unleashed that would sweep up everything in its path.

An unbidden image of him naked exploded in her mind, stirring a prickle of sensation deep down inside her. It wasn't fear and that scared her even more.

'Scent aside…' he tilted his head '…which, by the way, I believe is Jenson's Floral Fantasy.'

How did he know that? She frantically glanced around, looking for a camera or any sign that this was some sort of a set-up, a joke being played on her because she was a new staff member, but she couldn't see anything. She turned back to him and his tight expression suddenly faded, replaced by a smile that crawled across his face, streaking up through jet stubble and crinkling the edges of his eyes. It lit up his aura of darkness and she wondered why she'd ever been scared of him.

His rich laugh had a bitter edge. 'I would need to be deaf not to hear the argument you were having with your feet.'

He knows you were scared.

Stung into speech, she tried for her most cutting tone—the one she knew put over-confident medical students in their place. 'I was *not* arguing with my feet.'

'Is that so? What else would you call that stop-start shuffle you were doing?'

'It was dark and I couldn't see.'

'Tell me about it.'

The harshness of his words crashed over her and still he kept staring. It was as if he could see not only her fear of the dark but so many other things that she kept hidden. His uncanny detective skills left her feeling vulnerable and exposed. She hated that and it harnessed her anger. 'Will you *stop* staring at me?'

He flinched and turned forty-five degrees. 'I apologise.'

The tension in his body was so taut she could have bounced a ball off it and his broad shoulders seemed to slice into the surrounding air. As ridiculous as it seemed, she got the impression she'd just insulted him. 'I'm sorry, that was rude. It's just I'm not used to meeting anyone down here at this time of the day and, as I said before, I got a fright.'

He didn't look at her. 'Please be assured I have no plans to rape, assault or hurt you in any way.'

The harsh edge of his voice did little to reassure her. She'd never met anyone who spoke so directly and without using the cover of social norms. 'I guess I'll take that in the spirit it's intended, then.'

'You do that.' A silence expanded between them and was only broken by his long sigh. 'The only reason I'm in this corridor is because it's the mirror image of every other corridor in this wing of The Harbour. If you were on level one, what would be on your left?'

She shook her head as if that might change his question. 'Is this some sort of test?'

'Something like that.'

His muttered reply didn't ease her confusion. 'Um, we're underneath the theatre suite.'

'We're standing directly under theatre *one*.' He almost spat the words at her.

She'd had enough. 'Look, Mr um…?'

'Jordan.'

'Okay, Jordan, I've been at The Harbour for a month, but you know this, right? You're in on some crazy initiation joke at my expense.'

He turned back to face her, his cheeks suddenly sharper. 'Believe me, none of this is a joke, Ms…?'

This was ridiculous. Everything about this encounter held an edge of craziness, including her reaction to him, which lurched from annoyance at his take-no-prisoners attitude to mini-zips of unwanted attraction. She closed the gap between them and extended her hand in her best professional manner. 'Grey. Hayley Grey. Surgical registrar.'

Sea-green eyes—the electric colour of the clear waters that surrounded a coral cay—bored into her, making her heart hiccough, but his hand didn't rise to meet hers. She dropped her gaze to his right hand and now she was closer she could see it gripped what looked like black sticks. With a jolt and a tiny but audible gasp, she realised it was an articulated cane.

Her cheeks burned hot. Oh, God, she'd just accused a blind man of staring at her.

Before she could speak, the doors to the car park opened and a young man wearing elastic-sided boots, faded jeans and a hoodie crossed the threshold and stood just inside the doors.

Jordan immediately turned toward the sound of cowboy heels on lino. 'Jared?'

'Yeah.' The young man grinned and shot Hayley an appreciative look that started at her head and lingered on her breasts.

Jordan turned back and this time his blind stare hit her shoulder. 'Now you have light, can I assume you're able to find your way to the car park alone?'

His tone managed to combine a minute hint of concern with a dollop of superciliousness and it undid any good intentions she had of apologising for her massive faux pas. Her chin shot up. 'I wouldn't dream of holding you up.'

'Goodbye, then, Hayley Grey.' He flicked out his cane, clicked his tongue and started walking.

She watched his retreating back and slow and deliberate stride as the clicks echoed back to him, telling him where the walls were.

As he approached the door he said, 'You're late, Jared.'

The young man jangled the keys in his hand. 'Sorry, Tom.'

Hayley froze. Tom? She'd thought his first name was Jordan.

Mr Jordan. Tom Jordan.

The conversation about the mysterious disappearance

of The Harbour's favourite neurosurgeon came back to her in a rush.

No way.

It had to be a coincidence. Both names were common. There'd have to be a thousand Thomas Jordans living and working in Sydney. But as much as she tried to dismiss the thought, the Tom Jordan she'd just met knew the hospital intimately. Still, perhaps one of those other thousand Tom Jordans worked at the hospital too. He could easily be an I.T guy.

We're standing directly under theatre one.

She might not know the complete layout of The Harbour, but she knew the theatre suite. Theatre one was the neurosurgery theatre, but the man walking away from her was blind. It was like trying to connect mismatching bits of a puzzle.

The man's gone to ground and doesn't want to be found.

And just like that all her tangled thoughts smoothed out and Hayley swallowed hard. She'd just met the infamous missing neurosurgeon, Tom Jordan, and he had danger written all over him.

CHAPTER TWO

Tom worked hard not to say anything to Jared about his driving as the car dodged and wove through the increasing rush-hour traffic. Tom knew this route from the hospital to his apartment as intimately as he knew the inside of a brain. In the past he'd walked it, cycled it and driven it, but he'd never been chauffeured. Now that happened all the time.

Being a passenger in a car had never been easy for him, even before he'd lost his sight. Whenever he'd got into a car he'd had an overwhelming itch to drive. Perhaps it was connected with the fact he'd grown up using public transport because his mother couldn't afford a car. Whatever the reason, he remembered the moment at sixteen, after a conversation with Mick and Carol, when he'd decided that one day he would own his own car. From his first wreck of a car at twenty, which he'd kept going with spare parts, to the Ferrari that Jared was driving now, he'd always been the one with his hands on the wheel, feeling the car's grip on the road and loving the thrum of the engine as it purred through the gear changes.

Tom stared out the side window even though he couldn't make out much more than shadows. 'Give cyclists a good metre.'

'Doing it. So, did you crash into anything this morning?'

Tom could imagine the cheeky grin on Jared's face—the one he always heard in the young man's voice whenever he'd given him unnecessary instructions. 'No, I didn't crash into any walls.'

'What about that woman you were talking to?'

Hayley Grey. A woman whose smoky voice could change in a moment from the trembling vibrato of fear to the steel of 'don't mess with me'. 'I didn't crash into her.'

'She looked pretty ticked off with you just as you left.'

'Did she?' He already knew she had been ticked off by his ill-mannered offer—an offer generated by the anger that had blazed through him the moment he'd heard her realisation that he was blind. He refused to allow anyone to pity him. Not even a woman whose voice reminded him of soul music.

Jared had just given him a perfect opportunity to find out more about her. Making the question sound casual, he asked, 'How exactly did she look?'

'Stacked. She's got awesome breasts.'

Tom laughed, remembering the gauche version of himself at the same age. 'You need to look at women's faces, Jared, or they're going to punch you.'

'I did start with her face, Tom, just like you taught me, but come on, we're guys, and I thought you'd want to know the important stuff first.'

And even though Jared was only twenty, he was right. When Tom had had his sight, he'd always appreciated the beautiful vision of full and heavy breasts. He suddenly pictured that deep, sensual voice with cleavage and swallowed hard. 'Fair enough.'

If Jared heard the slight crack in Tom's voice he didn't mention it. 'She's tall for a chick, got long hair but it was tied back so I dunno if it's curly or straight, and she's kinda pretty if you like 'em with brown hair and brown eyes.'

Knowing Jared's predilection for brassy blondes, Tom instantly disregarded the 'kinda'.

'Her nose wasn't big but it wasn't small neither but her mouth…' Jared slowed to turn.

A ripple of something akin to frustration washed through Tom as he waited for Jared to negotiate the complicated intersection he knew they'd arrived at. The feeling surprised him as much as the previous rush of heat. He hadn't experienced anything like that since before the accident. Even then work had given him more of a rush than any woman ever had—not that he'd been a recluse. He'd had his fair share of brief liaisons, but he'd always ended them before a woman could mention the words, 'the future'.

The car turned right, changed lanes and then took a sharp left turn. Tom's seat belt held him hard against the seat as they took a steep descent toward the water and his apartment. He broke his code and said, 'What about her mouth?'

'Her mouth was wide. Like it was used to smiling, even though it wasn't smiling at you.'

'I gave her a fright.' He wasn't admitting to more than that.

He heard the crank of the massive basement garage door opening, and as Jared waited for it to rise, Tom assembled all the details he'd just been given, rolling them around in his mind, but all he got was a mess of body parts. It was a pointless exercise trying to 'identikit' a picture because all of it was from Jared's perspective.

His gut clenched. He'd lost his job, his career and, damn it, now all he ever got was other people's perspectives.

Stick with what you know.

His ears, nose and skin had become his eyes so he concentrated on what he'd 'seen'. Hayley Grey was a contradiction in terms. Her fresh scent of sunshine and summer gardens said innocence and joy, but it was teamed with a voice that held such depth he felt sure it had the range to sing gut-wrenching blues driven by pain.

'Tom, Carol rang from Fiji. She said, "Good luck with today, not that you'd need it." I told her you'd call her back. She's sort of like a mum, isn't she?'

'Sort of.' He smiled as he thought of Carol working with kids in the villages, glad she'd actually respected his wishes and had not come rushing back to Sydney when he'd finally told her about the accident and his blindness. She'd be back in a few weeks, though.

Thinking about Carol's message grounded him—centring him solidly where he needed to be: in the present. Reminding him he had far more important things to be thinking about than a surgical registrar. Just like before he'd lost his sight, work came ahead of women and now he had even more of a reason to stick to that modus operandi. Sure, he'd given the occasional lecture before he'd gone blind, but he wasn't known for his lecturing style. No, he'd been known for a hell of a lot more.

What was the saying? 'Those who can, do, and those who can't, teach.' Bitterness surged. Lecturing was hardly going to set the world on fire. The accident had stolen so much from him and was now forcing him to do something that didn't come naturally, but until he worked out if he was staying in medicine or not, it was all that was open to him. He couldn't fail. He wouldn't allow that to happen, especially not in front of his previous colleagues.

He wasn't afraid of hard work—hell, he'd been working hard since he was fourteen and Mike had challenged him to improve at school so he could stay on the football team. His goals had changed, but his way of achieving them had not—one hundred per cent focus on the job at hand with no distractions from any other quarter. This morning's trip to SHH had been all about navigating his way around the hospital in preparation for his first lecture. He was determined to show everyone at The Harbour that although his domain had changed and had been radically curtailed, he was still in charge and in control, exactly as he'd been two years ago.

Jared was his sole concession in acknowledging that with driving he required assistance. The fact that Jared had turned up in Perth and refused to leave had contributed to the decision.

'I've got two lectures. One at one p.m. and the other at six.' Tom hoped he'd hidden his anxiety about the lectures, which had been rising slowly over the last two days. 'I'll need you to set up the computer for me both times.'

He heard Jared's hesitation and his concerns rose another notch. 'Is there a problem with that?'

'You know I'd do anything for you, Tom.'

And he did. He'd saved Jared's life and now Jared was making his life more tolerable.

'I've got a chemistry test at six and I asked the teacher if I could sit it with the full-time students, but that's the same time as your lecture.'

It had taken Tom weeks to convince Jared to return to school and he wasn't going to let him miss the test, even though it meant he was going to have to ask for assistance from The Harbour. He swallowed against the acrid taste in his mouth that burned him every time he had to ask for anything. 'You can't miss a chem test if you want to get into medicine.'

'Yeah, but what if someone sets up your computer all wrong?'

Tom gave a grim smile. 'They wouldn't dare.'

'Push fluids!' Evie Lockheart tried not to let the eviscerating scream of the monitors undo her nerve. She had a patient with a flail chest and she knew without the shadow of a doubt that he was bleeding, but from where exactly she was yet to determine.

'See this bruise?' She hovered the ultrasound doppler over her patient's rigid abdomen.

James, a final-year medical student, peered at it. 'From a seat belt?'

'Yes. So we're starting here and examining the spleen and the liver first.'

'Even though he's got a haemothorax?'

'With his pressure barely holding, we're looking for a big bleed.'

Everyone stared at the grainy black-and-white images on the small screen. 'There it is.' Evie froze the frame. She pointed to a massive blood clot. 'Ruptured liver, and they bleed like a stuck pig. He needs to go to—'

'Why the hell isn't this patient upstairs yet?'

Evie's team jumped as Finn Kennedy, SHH's head of surgery, strode into the resus room, blue eyes blazing and his face characteristically taut under the stubble of a two-day growth. His glare scorched everyone.

'Catheterise our patient,' Evie instructed the now trembling James, before flicking her gaze to Finn. He looked more drawn than usual but his gaze held a look of combat.

In the past she might have thought to try and placate him, but not now. Not after the night he'd obviously spent with Suzy Carpenter, the nurse from the OR who had the

reputation of sleeping with any male who had MD after
his name. That Finn had slept with that woman only a few
hours after what they'd both shared in the locker room left
her in no doubt that she, Evie, meant nothing to Finn.

She lifted her chin. 'If you want him to bleed out in the
lift on the way to Theatre, by all means take him now.'

'It looks like he's doing that here.'

'He's more stable than he was ten minutes ago when
his pressure was sixty over nothing.'

'Better to have him on the table stopping the bleeding
than down here pouring fluids into a leaky bucket.'

'Five minutes, Finn.' She ground out the words against
a jaw so tight it felt like it would snap.

His eyes flashed brilliant blue with shards of silver
steel. 'Two, Evie.'

'Catheter inserted, Ms Lockheart.'

'Excellent.'

'Packed cells.' A panting junior nurse rushed in, holding the lifesaving red bags aloft.

'Check O positive.'

'Check O positive.' The nurse stabbed the trocar
through the seal and adjusted the flow.

'Ninety on sixty. Good job, people. James, get the lift,'
Evie instructed, before turning to Finn. 'He's all yours.'

'About damn time.' Finn kicked off the brakes of the
trolley and started pushing it despite the fact that the nurse
was putting up a bag of saline. 'Move it, people!'

A minute later Evie stood in the middle of the resus
room with only the detritus of the emergency as company. She could hear Finn barking instructions and knew
the nurses and the hapless med student would be shaking
in their shoes. The staff feared Finn Kennedy. She had
been the one SHH staff member to see a different side
of him—the one where she'd glimpsed empathy and ten-

derness—yet it had been shadowed by overwhelming and gut-wrenching pain.

She swallowed hard as she remembered back to their moment of tenderness in the locker room two weeks ago after one of the worst days of her career. How he'd leaned back into her, how she'd rested her head against his shoulder blade and they'd just stood, cradled together as one with understanding flowing between them. Understanding that life can be cruel. Understanding that some days fear threatened to tear you down. Understanding each other.

Hope had flared inside her, along with flickering need.

And then he'd slept with Suzy.

Don't go there. She bent down and picked up the discarded sterile bag that had held the intravenous tubing and absently dropped it into the bin. It wasn't her job to clean up but she needed to keep moving and keep busy because thinking about Finn made her heart ache and she hated that. She wouldn't allow it. Couldn't allow it. Letting herself care for Finn Kennedy would be an act of supreme stupidity and if growing up as a Lockheart had taught her anything, it was that being self-contained was a vital part of her life.

'Move the damn retractor,' Finn yelled. 'It's supposed to be helping me see what I'm doing, not blocking me.'

'Sorry.' James hastily moved the retractor.

Finn wasn't in the mood for dealing with students today. Two minutes ago he'd made an emergency midline incision and blood had poured out of the patient's abdomen, making a lake on the floor. As he concentrated on finding the source of the bleeding, pain burned through his shoulder and down his arm, just as it had done last night and most every other night. It kept him awake and daylight hadn't soothed it any. Even his favourite highland malt whisky hadn't touched it.

'Pressure's barely holding, Finn.' The voice of David, the anaesthetist, sounded from behind the sterile screen. 'Evie did a great job getting him stable for you.'

'Humph.' Finn packed more gauze around the liver. He sure as hell hadn't been in the mood to see Evie. The sharp tilt of her chin, the condemning swing of her honey-brown hair, which matched the reproving glance from those warm hazel eyes, had rammed home how much he'd hurt her the night he'd slept with that nurse from OR.

He'd had no choice.

You always have a choice. You chose to hurt her to protect yourself.

The truth bit into him with a guilt chaser. Giving in and letting his body sink into Evie's and feeling her body cradling his had been one of those things that just happened between two people in the right place at the right time, but the rush of feeling it had released had been wrong on so many levels. Letting people get close had no value. It just paved the way to heartache and despair, so he'd done what he'd needed to do. But a kernel of guilt burrowed in like a prickly burr, and it remained, making him feel uncomfortable, not just for Evie but for the nurse, whose name he couldn't remember.

Finn grunted his thanks as the surgical registrar kept the suction up while he zapped another bleeder. The blood loss appeared to be easing, and with the patient's pressure holding he was confident he was winning the battle. 'You're new. Who are you?'

Tired eyes—ones that could match his for fatigue and lack of sleep—blinked at him for a moment from above the surgical mask. 'Hayley Grey. I've been at The Harbour a few weeks, but mostly on nights.'

More blood pooled. His chest tightened. God, this liver was a mess. 'I don't need your life story.'

She spoke quietly but firmly. 'I'm not giving it. This is my final rotation. By the end of the year I should be qualified.'

'You hope. The exam's a bastard.' The packs around the liver were soaked again. 'More packs.' He removed the old ones and blood spurted up like a geyser. Monitors screamed with deafening intent.

'Hell, Finn, what did you do?' David's strained voice bounced off the theatre walls. 'More blood. Now.'

'It's under control.' But it wasn't. Blood loss like this only meant one thing—a torn hepatic vein. Damn it, the packs had masked it and he'd been dealing with minor bleeders as a result. He pushed the liver aside and gripped the vein between his thumb and forefinger. 'David, I'm holding the right hepatic vein shut until you've got some more blood into him.' He raised his gaze to his pale registrar. 'Ever seen a rapid trauma partial liver resection?'

She shook her head. 'Will you use a laser?'

'No time.' With his left hand he pointed to a tear in the liver. 'I learned this in the army. We start here and do a finger resection. I can have that liver into two pieces in thirty seconds.' He was gripping the vein so hard that his thumb and index finger started to go numb. 'Ready, David?'

'One more unit.'

'Make it quick.' He pressed his fingers even harder, although he couldn't feel much. 'I'll need a clamp and 4-0 prolene.'

'Ready.' The scrub nurse opened the thread.

'Be fast, Finn.' There was no masking of the worry in the anaesthetist's voice.

'I intend to be. Keep that sucker ready, Ms Grey.'

He released his grip and slid his fingers through the liver. The expected tingling of his own blood rushing into his numb fingers didn't come. They continued to feel thick and heavy. 'Clamp!'

He grabbed it with his left hand and saw surprise raise the scrub nurse's brows.

'Hurry up, Finn,' David urged. 'Much longer and there'll be more blood in the suction bottle than in the patient.'

Blood spewed, the scream of monitors deafened and sweat poured into his eyes. *You're losing him.* 'Just do your job, David, and I'll do mine.' He snarled out the words as he managed to apply the clamp.

He flexed his fingers on his right hand, willing the sensation to return to his thumb and index finger. He could do some things with his left hand but he couldn't sew. He accepted the threaded needle from the scrub nurse and could see the thread resting against the pad of his thumb. He couldn't feel it. With leaden fingers he started to oversew the vein but the thread fell from his numb fingers. He cursed and tried to pick it up but the lack of sensation had him misjudging it. He dropped it again.

Another set of fingers entered the field, firmly pushing the sucker against his left palm and deftly picking up the thread. With a few quick and dexterous flicks, the registrar completed the oversewing before taking back the suction.

Finn's throat tightened and he swallowed down the roar of frustrated fury that she'd taken over. That she'd needed to take over. He barked out, 'Remove the clamp.'

Hayley removed the clamp. All eyes stared down.

The field mercifully stayed clear of blood.

'Lucky save, Finn,' said David from behind the screen.

Except David hadn't seen who'd stopped the bleeding.

Brown eyes slowly met Finn's but there was no sign of triumph in the registrar's gaze, or even a need for recognition that she'd been the one to save the patient. Instead, there was only a question. One very similar to the query he'd seen on Luke's face. And on Evie's.

Don't go there. He stared at Hayley. 'And next, Ms Grey?'

'We complete the resection of the right side of the liver?'

'And you've done that before?'

'I have, yes, during elective surgery.'

The pain in his arm grew spikes and the numbness in his finger and thumb remained. Any hope that it would fade in the next few minutes had long passed. 'Good. You're going to do it again.' He stepped back from the table and stripped off his gloves then spoke to remind her of hospital protocol.

'Oh, and, Ms Grey, as surgical registrar you must attend the series of lectures that start today. They count toward your professional hours. Your log book needs to be verified and notify my secretary of the conferences you wish to attend so they can be balanced off with the other registrars' requirements.'

He didn't wait for a reply. As chief of surgery it was his prerogative to leave closing up to the minions. The fact that today he'd needed to scared him witless.

Hayley accepted the tallest and strongest coffee the smiling barista said she could make and hoped the caffeine would kick in fast. The plan for the day had been to sleep and arrive just in time for the six o'clock lecture, but the moment her head had hit the pillow she'd been called in to work again due to a colleague's illness. This time she'd found herself scrubbed in with the chief of surgery. Finn

Kennedy was everything everyone said—tall, brusque and brilliant. The way he'd finger-dissected their patient's liver to save his life had been breathtaking. But his gruff manner and barked commands made it impossible to relax around him. Cognisant of the fact that he was her direct boss, she'd been determined to make a good impression. Ironically, she'd effectively killed that idea by acting on pure instinct and taking over in mid-surgery when he hadn't been able to make the closure. She'd fully expected Mr Kennedy to order her out of his theatre, but instead he'd been the one to leave. She wondered if she'd be reprimanded later.

Probably. She sighed, not wanting to think about it, so she set it aside like she did a lot of things—a survival habit she'd adopted at eleven. She'd deal with it if it ever happened. Right now, she needed to deal with no sleep in twenty-four hours and staying awake through an hour-long lecture. Some of the lecturers were so dry and boring that even when she wasn't exhausted she had trouble staying awake. She'd been so busy operating she hadn't even caught up with the topic, but she hoped it was riveting because otherwise she'd be snoring within five minutes.

Gripping her traveller coffee mug, she walked toward the lecture theatre and stifled a slightly hysterical laugh.

She'd always known that training to become a surgeon would be a tough gig and she wasn't afraid of hard work, but it had become apparent that operating was the easy part of the training. It was all the lectures, tutorials, seminars and conferences that came on top of her regular workload that made it unbelievably challenging. Even with all the extra work and the fact she had no desire for a social life, she could have just managed to cope, but lately her chronic insomnia, which she'd previously be able to manage, was starting to get on top of her. Had she been able to get more than three hours' sleep in twenty-four she could function, but that wasn't possible now she had to work more days than nights. She preferred night work, but as she was in her final year, she needed more elective surgery experience, which meant working more days.

She paused outside the lecture theatre, wondering why the foyer was so quiet, and then she glanced at her watch. She was early. No matter, she'd take the opportunity to hide up at the back of the lecture hall and take a quick ten-minute power-nap. She'd doze while she waited for the coffee to kick in. Her colleagues always used the dark on-call room but for her the brighter the light, the better she slept. She gripped the heavy door's handle and pulled.

Tom heard the click of the door opening and immediately breathed in the heart-starting aroma of strong, black coffee. A buzz of irritation zipped through him. Had the IT guy stopped for coffee, even though he'd already kept him waiting for fifteen minutes? Tom had deliberately booked him half an hour earlier than his lecture start time to avoid any stress on the run-up to the Jared-less evening lecture, but right now he could feel his control of the situation slipping due to his unwanted dependence on others. He tried to clamp down on the surge of frustration that filled him, but it broke through his lips.

'It's about damn time. I've attempted to connect the computer myself, but there's no sound.' The person didn't reply and Tom turned, seeking out the shadowy outline. As he did, he caught the hint of an undertone of a floral scent. A very feminine scent. He let out a low groan. 'You're not the IT guy, are you?'

'Should I be?'

'I would have preferred it.'

'Sorry to disappoint you.'

Her seductively husky voice, edged with a touch of sarcasm, swirled around him, leaving him in no doubt he was speaking to Hayley Grey. An image of soft, creamy breasts exploded in his head and he tried to shake it away. 'That's hellishly strong coffee you're drinking.'

'It's been a hellish kind of a day.' She sighed as if standing in the lecture hall was the last place on earth she wanted to be.

He knew exactly how that felt.

'Do you need a hand, Mr Jordan?'

I need eyes. He forced his clenched fingers to relax and ran them over his braille watch, realising that the IT technician was now twenty minutes late. Need won out over pride. 'Do you know anything about computers?'

A lilting laugh washed over him. 'I can turn one on and off.'

'I suppose I'll have to work with that, then.' God, he hated incompetence and right now he was ready to lynch the absent IT professional. It was bad enough having to ask for help let alone be supported by someone who didn't have the skills he needed. 'Can you follow instructions?'

He heard her sharp intake of breath at his terse question. 'I can follow *civil* instructions, yes.'

He found himself unexpectedly smiling. He couldn't remember the last time someone had spoken back to him and just recently most people—with the exception of Jared—tiptoed around him, making him want to scream. 'Good. We're in business, then. Follow me.'

He used his cane to tap his way to the lectern because when he was stressed he didn't do echolocation at all well, and falling flat on his face in front of Hayley Grey or anyone else from The Harbour wasn't going to happen. 'I can see light on the screen so I assume the picture is showing?'

'Your screensaver is. Nice picture.' Genuine interest infused her voice. 'Is that the Ningaloo Reef in Western Australia?'

He had no clue which one of his pictures Jared was currently using and he really didn't care. 'Probably.' He ran his hands around his computer until his fingers located the cord he knew he'd plugged into the sound jack. 'Is this green?'

'Yes.'

'Look on the lectern. Have I plugged it into a matching green jack?'

He felt strands of her hair brush his cheek as she leaned past him and this time he caught the scent of coconut and lime. It took him instantly to a beach in the tropics and for some crazy reason he thought of a bright red bikini and a deep cleavage. He felt a tightening against his pants.

It had been so long since anything had stirred in that region of his body that part of him was relieved it still all worked. Most of him wasn't.

Stop it. Concentrate on work.

Out of habit, he closed his eyes to rid himself of the image. The irony hit him hard—the only images he saw now were in his imagination and darkness didn't affect them one little bit.

'You only missed by one.'

The admiration in her voice scratched him. Once he'd been admired around the world for groundbreaking brain surgery. Now he needed help with basic technology. 'Just push the damn plug into the damn jack.'

He thought he heard her mumble, 'I'd like to plug it somewhere else.' A moment later music blared through the speakers. 'Good. It works.'

'So it does.' She paused as if she expected him to say

something. Then she sighed again. 'If that's all, I'll leave you to it.'

Her tone reminded him he should thank her, but it was bad enough having to ask for help without then having to be permanently grateful. He almost choked on a clipped 'Thank you'.

'Any time.' Her polite response held a thread of relief that she could now leave and that 'any time' really meant 'not any time soon'.

He could hear the clack of heels and the firm tread of rubber as people entered the auditorium in large numbers. There'd been a reason his first lecture earlier in the day had been to the medical students. He'd warmed up on a less demanding audience—practised even—but now his colleagues were filing in and taking their seats. Some had come to hear him speak, some had come merely to confirm if the rumour that he was now blind was true, and he knew that a small number of people he'd ticked off over the years would have come to gloat that the mighty Tom Jordan had taken one of life's biggest falls.

His right hand fisted. He would not fail in front of them. Even when he'd been sighted he'd known how fickle technology could be and there was no way was he going to have an equipment stuff-up or malfunction that he couldn't see. He would not stand alone at the front of the theatre, hearing twitters of derision or pity.

He checked the time again with his fingers, and his chest tightened. The IT person still hadn't arrived and Jared's worst-case scenario had just come true. He thought of how he'd once commanded a crack team of surgeons, nurses and allied health professionals, and how their groundbreaking surgery had made headlines around the world. He'd demanded perfection but he'd never asked for anything.

But *everything* in his life had changed and he was being dragged kicking and screaming in the slipstream. His throat tightened and he gripped the lectern so hard the edge bit into his palm, but that pain was nothing compared to what was about to happen. Summoning up steely determination, he made himself say the words he never wanted to utter. 'I need you to stay and be my eyes.'

CHAPTER THREE

'I'M NOT saying there weren't moments when I thought that the surgery might result in brain damage. In fact, there were many such moments, but as a surgical team we were committed to trying to offer these little twin boys, conjoined at the head since birth, a better life.'

Hayley listened spellbound as Tom Jordan's deep and confident voice boomed through the speakers while he presented his most groundbreaking neurological case. Something fell on her feet and with a rush of surprise she realised the printed version of his presentation had slipped off her lap. Initially, she'd done as Tom had asked and had turned each page of the document when he'd pressed his remote control to change the slide on the screen. This meant that she would know exactly what slide he was up to should something go awry with the computer, the data projector or the microphone.

Tom had been brusquely specific about the job he'd imposed on her, making her repeat his instructions back to him as if she was a child and not a nearly qualified surgeon. She'd almost told him to stick his lecture notes where 'the sun don't shine', but the edge of anxiety that had dared to hover around his commanding, broad shoulders had made her stay.

It hadn't taken long before she'd become so caught up

in the story and the technicalities of the surgery that she'd forgotten all about page turning. Instead, she was having a series of mini-moments of hero-worship as the implications of what Tom Jordan and his team had achieved sank in. It had been the 'moon landing' of surgeries.

'This surgery was the culmination of two years of work, and innovation was key.' Tom stared at the back of the room as he spoke. 'Not only were we successful, we paved the way for other neurosurgeons, and earlier this year a similar operation took place in the UK.'

She leaned down, picking up the folder, and then glanced up at Tom. The tense, angry and pedantic man who'd greeted her earlier was gone. In his place was a brilliant surgeon, his long, lean and tanned fingers resting purposely on his braille notes. Notes he didn't need because she knew he could 'see' the surgery. At this very moment he was inside those little boys' brains, and his passion for their well-being and giving them the chance at a normal life filled the auditorium, along with a sense of humility that he and his team had been given such an opportunity.

There was nothing dry and dusty about Tom Jordan and he held the silent audience in the palm of his hand. No one was nodding off to sleep or fiddling with their phone or doodling. Everyone was leaning forward, interested and attentive, and fascinated by the report of brilliant surgery told in an educative yet entertaining style.

All too soon the lecture was over and Hayley felt a zip of disappointment. She could have listened to Tom for a lot longer, but after he'd fielded questions for fifteen minutes he wound it all up. People started to leave and although some lingered for a moment as if they wanted to speak with Tom, most left without talking to him, their faces

filled with a mixture of sympathy and embarrassment—
what did you say to someone who'd lost their career?

Finn Kennedy stopped and gave his usual curt greeting before moving off quickly when Evie stepped up with Theo. Both of them greeted Tom warmly and as they departed, two men passed and started chatting to each other before they were out of earshot. 'Damn shame. He was the best and now—'

Hayley saw Tom's shoulders stiffen.

He heard them.

Of course he'd heard—the man had almost bionic hearing. She rushed to speak in the hope of drowning out the thoughtless remarks. In her post-lecture awe, she spoke more loudly than she intended. 'That was amazing.'

Tom flinched and turned toward her, his face granite. 'I'm blind, Hayley, not deaf.'

'I realise that, it's just that…' She didn't think he'd take kindly to her saying she'd had a crazy urge to protect his feelings when he didn't seem to have any problem with trampling on hers. *Stick to the surgery topic.* 'I was in the UK when I heard about that surgery. I didn't realise it was you who'd led the team.'

'So now you know.' He turned away from her and pushed down the lid of his laptop with a sharp snap.

Her mind was flying on the inspirational lecture and the fact she was in the presence of the man the world media had declared 'a trailblazer'. 'It must have been the most incredible buzz when you realised you'd pulled it off.'

His generous mouth pulled into a grim smile. 'It's something you never forget.'

'I bet. I would have loved to have been there and seen you operating.'

His hands stilled on the laptop case. '*That* chance is long gone.'

A tingle of embarrassment shot through her. 'Sorry. I didn't mean to remind you that…' *Oh, God, oh, God, shut up!* She closed her eyes and stifled a groan. She'd managed to wrong-foot herself twice in two minutes.

'You didn't mean to remind me that I can no longer operate? How very thoughtful and considerate of you, Hayley.'

His sarcasm stung like the tail of a whip and this time she was the one to flinch. 'I think I need to start over. What I was trying to say was that your lecture was the best one I've heard. Ever heard.' She smiled and tried to joke. 'And, believe me, I've heard a lot of boring lectures in the last ten years. You're a gun lecturer and The Harbour's fortunate to have you.'

He slung his laptop bag abruptly across his chest. 'Aw, shucks. Stop now, you're embarrassing me.'

But his icy tone sounded far from embarrassed and with a wicked flick he extended his cane. She jumped sideways, narrowly avoiding being hit.

'I'm so glad that you're honouring me with the title of "gun" lecturer,' he continued. 'I mean, after all, that's what the last twenty years of my life have been about. Forget neurosurgery. Forget saving lives or improving lives and lessening pain. All of that pales into insignificance compared to giving a *gun lecture*, especially to a group of people who'll probably never come close to achieving the level of technical expertise I was known for.' He started walking. 'But you wouldn't understand that, Hayley.'

His words fired into her like a shot, and she crossed her arms to stop herself from trembling from his unexpected verbal assault. To stop herself shaking from an incandes-

cent fury that was fuelled by his deliberate misconstruc-
tion of her sentiments, and his belief that he alone had
suffered in life. She knew far too intimately about loss
and how life went on regardless.

He was blind, not dead, and she wasn't treading carefully around him any more. 'Were you this rude before
you went blind?'

He stopped walking and his roared reply echoed around
the now empty auditorium. 'I was a neurosurgeon.'

She swayed at the blast. 'I'll take that as a "yes", then.'

For a moment he didn't speak. His sightless emerald
eyes continued to stare at her but his previously hard expression had softened a touch. 'Out of curiosity, Hayley,
are you new to The Harbour because you were asked to
leave your last post?'

As a woman in the very male-dominated world of surgery, she'd learned early to stand her ground. Something
told her this was the only approach with the darkly char-
ismatic Tom Jordan. Her chin shot up. 'My recommenda-
tions from The Royal in London make the paper they're
written on glow in the dark.'

She waited for a sarcastic put-down but a beat went by
and then he laughed. A big, bold, deep laugh that made
his eyes crinkle up at the edges and sparkle like the sea
on a sunny day.

'Which is why I imagine you got a coveted surgical
registrar's position at The Harbour.'

She dropped her arms by her sides and relaxed slightly,
knowing his statement was as close as a man like Tom
Jordan would ever come to a compliment. 'It was the
top of my list because of its association with Parkes
University.'

'Mine too.' His brows drew down for a moment and
then he seemed to throw off the frown. 'You said before

you had a hellish day and mine, as you've adroitly de-
duced, wasn't much better. How about we end it in a more
pleasant way and I buy you dinner?'

Shocked surprise sent her blood swooping to her toes
and was instantly followed by a flare of heat. *Dinner?*
The idea of dinner with Tom Jordan the surgeon delighted
her because she'd love to hear more about his pioneering
operations. The idea of dinner with Tom Jordan the man
didn't generate quite the same feelings. An evening of
verbal sparring would be exhausting and she was already
beyond tired, but there was also a tiny part of her that was
intrigued. He was heart-stoppingly handsome, just as the
nurses had told her, but his soul had a shadow on it darker
than his cocoa-coloured hair. That was enough to warn
her that dinner wasn't a good idea.

That and the fact that she generally didn't date.

Vacillating, she bit her lip. 'That's very kind of you
but—'

'But what?' The thin veneer of politeness that covered all that raw energy and 'take no prisoners' attitude
cracked yet again.

She almost snapped at him and said, 'Because of that',
but as she opened her mouth she saw a different tension in
his jaw. *He's expecting you to say no.* The thought made
her stomach squirm. Did he really think she'd reject his
invitation because he was blind?

Rude, yes, blind, no.

She thought of all the people at the lecture who'd known
him when he'd been head of neurosurgery and who'd pre-
varicated and then chosen not to speak to him because
they didn't know what to say to the man who'd once held
the pinnacle of all surgery positions. She wouldn't do that
to him even if the thought of dinner came more under the
banner of duty than pleasure.

Decision made, she pulled her shoulders back. 'I was going to say I'm not really dressed for dinner.'

'Dressed or naked makes no difference to me, but I assume you have clothes on.'

Her breasts tingled at the lazy way his mouth roved over the word 'naked' and she was thankful he couldn't see her pebbled nipples pushing against her T-shirt. As she tried to get her wayward body back under control she managed to splutter out an inane 'Of course I've got clothes on.'

His brows rose and he extended his arm. 'Then you're dressed for dinner. Hurry up before I change my mind.'

She rolled her eyes but slid her arm under his. His fingers immediately curved around her elbow, his warmth seeping through her long-sleeved T-shirt. 'I'm completely bowled over by your charm.'

'Of course you are.'

He smiled at her and her knees sagged. Dimples carved through evening stubble, changing everything about him. The hard planes of his face yielded to the softer lines of humour, light replaced dark and bitter gave way to sweet. Everything inside her melted. *What have I just gone and done?*

The sarcastic, bitter man was easy to resist. This more human version of Tom Jordan—not so much.

What the hell possessed you?

Now that Tom was seated opposite Hayley at Warung Bali, a casual restaurant a short walk from the hospital, the reality of inviting her to dinner hit him hard. He'd shocked himself with the unanticipated invitation, which had come out of nowhere. One minute he'd been livid with the injustice of everything that had happened to him and not being able to operate, and the next he'd found himself smiling and the anger had faded slightly.

Still, dinner?

Yes, that had probably been overkill, but after the lecture, part of him had wanted to hold on to something that resembled normality. Before blindness had stolen more than his sight, he'd often dated and more than once he'd taken a nurse or a resident for an impromptu drink at Pete's. He'd avoided Pete's tonight because revisiting the social hub of The Harbour on 'half-price Wednesdays' would have been more than he could bear.

The reaction of the medical students to his lecture at lunchtime had been in stark contrast to that of his colleagues this evening. It had taken him close to an hour to deal with the number of students who'd wanted to speak to him at the end of the lecture. Only a few of his previous colleagues had made themselves known to him and he understood why. If his career had been chopped off at the knees from one act of fate, then so could theirs be, and it terrified them. So they'd avoided him.

Now he was avoiding them.

He'd brought Hayley to this restaurant because he often ate here and it was a short walk from his apartment. Prior to tonight, he'd only ever eaten here alone so he hadn't anticipated that Wayan, the owner, would give Hayley such a rapturous welcome and offer champagne.

Tom had quickly gone into damage control. This wasn't a date. It was just a meal with a fellow doctor and an attempt at reality—nothing more, nothing less. In the past, he'd rarely taken anyone out more than once so the chances of this ever being repeated were exceedingly slim.

'Hayley is a colleague at the hospital, Wayan.'

'Hello, Wayan.' Her smoky voice had been infused with

warmth. 'As much as the idea of champagne is tempting, I'm on call and iced water would be wonderful.'

They'd discussed the menu, ordered their food, which had arrived promptly, and the pungent bouquet of lemon grass, coriander, peanut satay and chilli hadn't disappointed. The flavours on his tongue matching the promise of the tantalising aroma. Wayan had placed the food on the table and as Tom had instructed him on his very first visit said, 'On your plate, satay's at twelve o'clock, rice at three and vegetables at nine.'

Both he and Hayley had eaten in relative silence with only an occasional comment about the food. When he'd finally balled his serviette and dropped it on his plate he heard the clink of ice against glass, but it wasn't the movement caused by someone taking a sip. It was more continuous and he knew Hayley was stirring with her straw and staring down at her drink, probably wondering why she'd come.

He understood totally.

He swallowed, knowing he needed to break the silence. He'd never seen the point of chitchat with no purpose and he sure as hell wasn't going to talk about the weather or the lecture he'd just survived. He thought about the first time he'd met her. 'How long have you been scared of the dark?'

She coughed as if she was choking and he realised he'd missed the moment she'd taken a sip.

'How long have you been blind?'

Again he found himself smiling. Three times in one day had to be a record. 'I take it that your fear of the dark is off the conversation list.'

'Is your blindness?'

He thought about it. 'Yes and no.'

Her blurry outline leaned forward. 'Okay, I'll cut you a

deal. If either of us asks a question that goes beyond what we're comfortable answering, we just say, "Enough."'

He'd never met anyone quite like her. Women usually wanted to know every little detail and got offended if he didn't tell all. This suggestion of hers, however, was perfect—conversation with a get-out-now option. 'You're on.'

'Good.' The table rocked slightly as if she was pressing her hands down on it. 'I've been scared of the dark since I was a child and *don't* tell me I should have grown out of it by now.'

The heartfelt punch behind her words hit him in the chest and left behind the trace of a question he could easily ignore. 'I've been living in the dark for two years after an urban four-wheel drive, complete with a dirt-free roo bar, ran me off my bike when I was in Perth for a conference. I slammed into the road headfirst.'

Flashes of memory flitted in colour across his mind. Memories he'd learned to control. 'Ironically, I'm told that my skin's healed perfectly and I don't have a single scar but the impact stole my sight.' He forced his hands to stay in his lap and not grip the edge of the table as he braced himself for the platitudes he'd grown used to hearing.

'That sucks.'

He blinked. She'd just done it again—defied convention. 'It more than sucks, and coming back to Sydney is proving to be—' *Never admit weakness.* He cut himself off before he said more than he intended.

'Challenging. Purposeful. A relief?' The words hung in the air, devoid of anything other than their natural sound.

'I'm not sure it's a relief.' He ran his fingers along the edge of the spoon Wayan had put on the table as his marker to find his drink which was on a coaster directly above it.

'Why did you come back?'

He shrugged, not really understanding the decision himself. 'There's something about the pull of home.'

'Family?' Her usually firm voice suddenly sounded faint.

He shook his head and tried not to think about his mother. 'No, but I grew up here.'

Understanding wove through her voice. 'And you worked at The Harbour. That's got to be a strong pull too.'

It was like a knife to his heart. 'Don't tell me that lecturing is as important as surgery because you know it doesn't even come close.'

He'd expected her to object but instead she gave a heartfelt sigh. He knew exactly what that sound meant. Before he'd thought it through he found himself saying, 'There's something about holding the scalpel just before you cut.'

'I know, right?' Animation played through her voice. 'There's an exhilaration that gives you this amazing feeling, but there's also some tiny ripples of concern because no matter how routine the operation, there's always the threat of the unknown.'

Her words painted the perfect picture, describing with pinpoint accuracy that *one* moment every surgeon experienced. The image floated around him but instead of bringing on a cloud of bitterness, it brought back the buzz. A buzz he hadn't known in two long years.

Hell, he missed talking with a colleague—with a fellow surgeon. Sure, he'd talked to doctors in the last two years, but he'd been the patient and those conversations had been very, very different. 'And in neurosurgery even the known can bite you.'

He felt a flutter of air against his face and his nostrils

flared at the softest soupçon of magnolia. He realised she'd leaned forward again.

'Even with an MRI?'

He responded to the interest in her voice. 'They're a brilliant roadmap, certainly, but just like a photograph often it's all about what isn't in the picture.'

'The human body being a variation on a theme.'

The enthusiasm in her voice pulled him in. 'Absolutely. I remember once when I'd—' The strident notes of techno music split the air.

'Sorry, that's my phone.' The noise was immediately silenced. 'Hayley Grey.'

Tom had no choice but to sit and overhear one side of a conversation. A conversation so familiar that he'd said similar words in the past at dinners, from his bed, in the car and on his bike.

Hayley sucked in a sharp breath. 'When…? A and E…? How many…? Five minutes… Okay, two, then. Call David Mendez… Bye.'

His pulse rate had inexplicably picked up. 'Problem?'

'Road trauma.' The scrape of her chair screeched, matching the urgency in her voice. 'I have to get back.'

He carefully moved his chair back a short distance and rose to his feet, hating it that he didn't know exactly where she was standing, although he could smell her—smell the exhilarating combination of her perfume mixed in with her heady aroma of excitement. The thrill of the unknown—a surgeon's addiction.

'Tom.' Her hand slipped into his, her skin soft, warm and fragrant.

A wave of heat hit him so hard he had to fist his other hand to stop it from reaching out and pulling her against him. It was like his body had just woken up from a long, deep sleep and was absolutely starving. He craved to trace every curve and swell of her body, and he hungered to learn if her body was as lush and as sexy as her voice promised it would be, as her summer garden scent taunted that it was.

She squeezed his hand. 'Thank you for the best satay I've tasted outside Asia.'

'No...' Huskiness clung to the word and he cleared his throat. 'No problem. I'll walk you back.'

'Thank you, but I have to run.'

He'd heard the regret in her voice before she'd even said the word. He couldn't run.

She quickly withdrew her hand. 'I won't ask if you're all right to get home because you'd probably bite my head off.'

He forced a smile against the cold grimness that was washing through him and leaving behind a film of bleakness on every part of him that it touched. 'You're right about that.'

'I'm right about a lot of things. Goodbye, Tom.'

'Good night, Hayley.'

He heard her rapid footsteps, the tinkle of the bell as the door opened, the jet of winter night air that raced in around his ankles, and then the thud of the heavy door closing. And she was gone, running down the street with adrenaline pumping through her veins and her mind alert with every diagnostic possibility.

And he couldn't even freaking escort her back to The Harbour, let alone be involved with the emergency.

His hands fumbled with fury as they sought the back of the chair and with a curse he sat down heavily and felt his hand collide with the plate. Cold rice squelched through his fingers. He swore again and pushed the plate away. A crash followed.

The disappointments of the day and the bitter fury that

had been his companion since the accident rolled back in like a king tide. With a gasp he realised their arrival meant they'd been absent. Gone for the hour he'd spent at dinner.

The hour you spent with Hayley.

But now every single feeling was back with a vengeance—stronger and more devastating than before. It swamped him with the reminder that his current life was a very poor relation to the one he'd lived before. It clawed at him, pulling him down and forcing him back toward the pit of despair he'd only half dug himself out of.

Hayley would be operating within the hour. She would be saving lives. And what was he doing? Sticking his hand in cold food and making a damn mess. He fought for his breath against a tight and frozen chest. So what if she smelled like summer sunshine or if the timbre of her voice stroked him like a hot caress, sending his blood direct to his groin? If attempting normality meant being reminded of everything he'd lost, he wasn't ever doing it again.

'Wayan!' He heard himself yell and didn't care that probably every other patron in the small restaurant was staring at him.

'Yes, Tom?'

'Bring me the rest of that bottle of red wine. Now.'

He intended to lose himself in Connawarra's finest merlot and forget everything about Hayley Grey.

CHAPTER FOUR

HAYLEY woke up slowly, blinking against the sunlight that streamed in through her open curtains, and stretched out with a sigh. The brighter the light, the better she slept, and today was an exceptionally sunny day. It was also her day off—a day she usually spent studying.

At high school she'd spent her weekends studying instead of partying, and that had continued through medical school. Now her days off often came during the week but the pattern hadn't changed. She'd sleep really late and then study well into the night until she fell asleep at her desk under the glow of her reading lamp. There she could get a few hours' sleep, unlike in her bed.

She threw back the covers and got up, padding directly to her small kitchen to make a huge pot of Earl Grey tea and a plate of hot, buttered toast. While she waited for the kettle to boil, she opened up her study planner to see what the next topic of revision was, only this time her usual buzz of enthusiasm didn't stir. Instead, she had an overwhelming urge to do something totally different with her day. An urge so unexpected that it swooped in and changed the shape of her loneliness.

She bit her lip. She was intimate with loneliness—it had been part of her from the moment death had stolen not only her twin sister's life but a part of her life too.

Over the years it had become a living thing—a constant companion—despite other friendships. She'd thrown herself into study and then work, and she enjoyed being part of a huge institution, but the empty space inside her had never filled. She'd tried a few times to be a girlfriend, but she'd never found the connection strong enough. Eventually she'd accepted that there was always going to be a space between her and others. Still, she was a healthy woman with needs like anyone else so in the past she'd settled on two 'friends with benefits' arrangements—one at university and another last year in the UK. Both men had eventually wanted more than she could offer so she'd let them go, and happily watched each of them fall in love with a woman they deserved. A woman who was whole and could love them the way she never could. Now she was back in Sydney she didn't have time for anything other than work and her exam preparation. She'd spent years working toward this exam so she could proudly hang up a brass plate with her name on it—Ms Hayley Grey. Surgeon. FRACS.

Finn Kennedy was right. The exam was a bastard and the pass rate first time round was very low. She was determined to pass on her first attempt and for that to happen, study must be her priority. *Nothing* was going to derail her from her goal.

You enjoyed having dinner with Tom Jordan.

The kettle boiled and she poured the water over the fragrant leaves and breathed in deeply. To her total and utter surprise, the quick dinner she'd shared with Tom hadn't been the horror she'd anticipated. Sure, Tom had his own set of demons, but the flipside meant he wasn't interested in hers. Added to that, his conversation style was in such sharp contrast to the usual 'first date' scene that it had been both refreshing and stimulating.

It was hardly a date.

I know that.

She quickly buttered her toast but she couldn't deny that Tom's rough-edged charisma and wickedly deep voice kept coming back to her at all times of the day and night, making her feel flustered and tingly all at the same time. God, maybe she did need to have sex with someone soon.

Tom Jordan is not that one.

And she knew that. Dark and brooding was not for her. She needed light. She needed sunshine and happiness, which was why the two men she'd chosen in the past had been benign in comparison with Tom's rugged cynicism. But the problem was, she'd glimpsed the man who was buried under all that anger and sadness, and she wanted to see him again.

Her cheeks suddenly burned when she thought about how during the emergency surgery three nights ago she'd asked Theo in a roundabout way where Tom lived.

'*You* had dinner with Tom Jordan?'

Theo's eyes had widened so much that Hayley had thought they would explode and she'd realised she'd just given out information to a hard-core gossip.

'Yes, and I had to dash back here. I was just wondering if he'd chosen the restaurant because it was close to his place. If I was blind, I think I'd stick to known places.'

Theo had nodded and said, 'His apartment's on the top floor of the Bridgeview Building. I can't believe that all this time he's been blind and living in Perth, and none of us knew. Did he say what happened?'

Hayley didn't like to gossip but as she'd been the one to bring the topic up she took the middle road. 'I only met the man this morning and he said he was knocked off his bike. I'm sure now that he's back in Sydney he'd appreciate a call from friends and he'll probably tell you a lot more that he did me.'

Theo had almost dropped the Yankauer sucker. 'Tom Jordan was incredibly well respected amongst the staff but he wasn't someone you made friends with or saw much outside the hospital. Believe me, many of the nurses tried but he pretty much held himself apart. Tom could talk surgery for hours, but put him in a staffroom with a group discussing last night's favourite TV show and it was like sticking him in a foreign country where he didn't speak the language. Put it this way, the man doesn't do small talk.'

How long have you been scared of the dark?

Hayley smiled at the recollection as she bit into the toast. Theo was right. Tom still didn't do small talk but, then again, neither did she—or when she tried she didn't do it very well. She totally understood what it was like to feel completely at sea when surrounded by an animated discussion about who would be eliminated next from the phenomenally popular cooking show on television. She hardly watched any TV and if she did have some downtime she tended to re-watch her favourite movies on DVD.

She gave herself a shake. Enough of straying thoughts and Tom Jordan. It was time to knuckle down to her day. But as she rinsed her plate and mug, the need to move, to do something different, intensified. It was as if her entire body was fidgeting. With a sigh she tossed the tea towel over the dish drainer.

Go for a run. She smiled at the thought. Exercise was the perfect solution to working off this unusual lack of focus and after a long run she'd be able to settle down to study.

Five minutes later and with her MP3 player strapped to her arm, she slipped a key into her pocket and headed out the door. She usually ran down towards Luna Park, but today she just started running, letting her feet take her wherever, and it didn't take long before she realised she was almost at the hospital. When she reached it, she ran along the back boundary, past Pete's and the crashing sound of bottles being thrown in the dumpster for recycling, and then across into the strip shopping centre. Dodging through the building lunchtime crowd, she automatically slowed as she passed Wayan's.

What are you doing? Tom won't be there.

She looked anyway.

Told you he wouldn't be there.

Shut up.

She continued the run, silencing the chatter in her head by pushing her body hard and turning her mind over to the demands of keeping one foot in front of the other until she reached a small park close to the sparkling waters of Sydney harbour. As always, the harbour was busy with yachts, motor launches and the ever-present green and yellow ferries that carried commuters all over Sydney. Panting, she stopped at a water fountain and quenched her thirst before leaning over a park bench and doing some necessary stretching. She'd taken a zigzag route from home but now she was at the lowest point. It was going to be a long, uphill climb all the way back.

Giving her body some recovery time, she walked slowly through the small park and came out on the high side, away from the water. It took her a moment to work out exactly where she was and then she saw the gold letters on the building in front of her. Bridgeview.

Tom's building?

She crossed the street and peered at the list of names next to the pad of doorbells. His name was at the top of the list. A zip of heat shot through her and without stopping to think she pressed her finger to the button.

Her brain instantly engaged. *What are you doing?* She pulled her finger off the button as if it was on fire, but it was too late. The peal of the electronic bell sounded back at her from the intercom.

'Did you forget your key, Jared?'

Horrified, she stared at the intercom.

'Jared?'

Say something or walk away. 'I'm not Jared.'

'Who is it?'

Tom's voice sounded deeper than ever through the intercom and her heart skipped a beat.

'It's, um…' *Oh, for heaven's sake, you know your own name.* She gave herself a shake and tried to settle the cotillion of butterflies that had taken over her stomach. 'Hayley.' She quickly added, 'Grey' for clarification, and then gave a silent groan of humiliation.

She stood there in her running gear, dripping in sweat and feeling incredibly foolish. What on earth had possessed her to ring his doorbell? Worse still, what was she going to say if he actually asked her why she was there? "Just passing. Thought I'd drop in…"

With a groan she rested her head against the wall and closed her eyes, lamenting the fact she hadn't thought this through at all and hating that she'd allowed her wayward body to make decisions for her. Meanwhile, the silence extended beyond the time it would take to reply and had moved from a polite pause into seriously uncomfortable nothingness.

Just go home.

She pushed off the wall and then jumped as the buzzing sound of amplified silence blared out of the speaker.

'Are you still there?' Tom demanded.

Say nothing. Pretend you've left. 'I am.'

'I suppose you'd better come up, then.'

Her lips twitched into a half-smile. As invitations went, it summed up Tom perfectly—direct and straight to the point.

The door buzz sounded for a long moment. *You're committed now so open the door.* After a short hesitation she bit her lip, pushed against the heavy glass and stepped into the foyer. A whisper-quiet lift whizzed her to the top floor and then she was standing in front of an ivory-coloured door. Tom's front door. As she knocked, another zip of panic ricocheted through her. Oh, God, what was she doing? She was hot, sweaty and probably bright red. She wiped her hands down her running shorts and for one purely selfish moment she was glad he was blind.

The door opened and Tom stood in front of her, his chocolate-noir hair spiked as if his hands had ploughed through it a thousand times and strands of silver caressed his temples. Deep lines pulled around his bright green eyes and bracketed his generous mouth, and the familiar aura of strain circled him. Today, instead of being dressed head to toe in what she'd assumed was his signature black, he wore dark brown cord, slim-fit pants, a white shirt with a button-down collar and a chocolate-brown moleskin jacket. His clothes were all perfectly colour-coordinated and although there was no sign of any tweed, he looked every inch a university professor. Not that he technically was one, but she wondered if one day in the future he might just choose that path. His ruffled hair added to the look, although Hayley knew that was all to do with him not being able to see, because there was *nothing* about Tom that was absent-minded.

She smiled. 'Hello, Tom.'

He didn't offer his hand but gave her a nod and stood back from the door. 'Come in.'

She stepped into his apartment and stopped abruptly, instantly struck by a sense of space. It took her a moment to realise this was because he had hardly any furniture and what he did have was spaced a good distance apart. She noticed dents in the carpet and realised that once there'd been a lot more furniture, but the side tables and coffee table had now gone. A glossy black grand piano was the only piece of non-essential furniture.

As if reading her mind, he said in a manner-of-fact voice, 'Less to bump into and no sharp corners, which are murder on shins.' He stretched his hands out in front of him. His palms collided with her breasts.

For a split second his fingers brushed across her skimpy Lycra running top. A rush of delicious tingles swooped through her breasts, making them push against her bra and filling the curve of his palm. The rest of her body moaned as a shiver of need rocked and coiled between her legs with a jealous throb.

Tom quickly dropped his hands and stepped backwards, colliding with the now-closed door. Pain and discomfiture streaked across his face before he spoke through tight lips. 'I apologise.'

She wanted to die on the spot. Not because he'd touched her breasts—that had been pure pleasure—but because she'd caused him embarrassment and hurt in his own home. 'Please, there's no need to apologise.'

His eyes deepened to moss green and there wasn't a trace of humour on his face. 'So you're happy with men you barely know touching your breasts, are you?'

Her chin shot up. 'No, of course not. It's just that—'

'What?' He folded his arms over his chest and glared ever so slightly to her left.

'Well, it was an accident. I should have given you more space by moving further into the room.'

He'd stepped forward while she was speaking, all predatory intent, and a sizzle of something very strong arced between them, draining her brain and making her sway towards him.

'I might be blind, Hayley, but, believe me, I'm still very much a man.'

He stood so close that she felt his low words vibrating against her face. She could smell the crisp, fresh scent of his cologne, which mocked her as it was in stark contrast to the dangerous currents of lust and leashed restraint that circled him.

Currents that circled her too, buffeting her and taunting her. She slowly raised her hand and placed it on his chest in the exact place he'd put his hand on hers. When she spoke, her voice came out slightly breathless. 'Not for one moment have I *ever* doubted you were a man.'

His nostrils flared as he breathed in deeply and for a moment his face shed its tension and his sightless eyes flared with the same need she knew burned hotly in hers. His hand touched her bare waist and she rose on her toes, ready to brush his lips with hers.

A heartbeat away from her kiss, he tensed under her palm. Without a word he lifted his hand away from her waist, peeled back her fingers from his body and with a firm grip put her hand back by her side.

A chill like an arctic wind cooled her from the inside out.

He took five careful steps away from her. 'Why are you here, Hayley?'

Because you fascinate me. Because my subconscious led me to you, knowing I would have fought it otherwise.

Neither reply would work so she thought on her feet,

making up a reason for a visit that had none. Ignoring the fact she wasn't dressed for lunch, she said, 'I had to leave abruptly the other night but today's my day off. I thought we could try lunch, only this time we can manage to finish an entire meal.'

His fingers flexed. 'I believe we'd both finished eating our meal before you had to leave.'

She laughed. 'But I didn't get dessert.' *Shut up.* The moment the words left her lips she wanted to bury her face in her hands. The quip was supposed to have come out light-hearted and breezy, but instead her body had betrayed her by dropping her voice to an alto purr, making her sound like she was trying to seduce him.

He instantly raised a brow, but not even a hint of a smile cracked the tension on his face. 'It might be your day off, Hayley, but I have to work. I'm giving an afternoon lecture.'

'Oh. Right.' It was crazy to feel so disappointed when a moment ago the idea for the invitation hadn't even existed. Perhaps it was because she'd enjoyed their dinner the other night or perhaps it was some other reason altogether, but she surprised herself by asking, 'What about tonight, then?'

He shook his head. 'I have a dinner with Eric Frobisher.'

Against growing regret, she made herself sound very casual. 'Perhaps another time, then? Consider it an open invitation between two friends.'

The shadows that dogged him darkened even more, placing his cheekbones in sharp relief. 'I don't think so.' He turned away from her, out toward the multimillion-dollar view. The one he couldn't see.

There was no ambiguity in his words or his stance. This was an unequivocal rejection.

He doesn't like you.

She stood staring at his back, feeling out of place and completely in the way. How had she got this so wrong? The other night they'd got along in a funny sort of way and a few moments ago an attraction had pulsed so strongly between them that every part of her still vibrated with the remnants of desire.

She couldn't possibly have imagined it all, could she? And yet right now every fibre of his being screamed at her to leave.

More than anything she wished the floor would open up and swallow her or that she could just wave a wand and vanish. If this was what happened when she gave in to impulsive thoughts then she was done with them. She stomped down hard on the new and unsettling feelings that had led her straight into this demoralising situation. Gulping in a steadying breath, she accepted she had to leave but, damn it, she was going to exit with grace, style and good manners.

Rolling her shoulders back, she said, 'If you regret your decision, the hospital switchboard can give you my number.'

He didn't turn around or say another word.

A spark of anger flared at his rudeness and total disregard for her feelings. 'I won't impose on you any longer. Goodbye, Tom. I'll let myself out.'

Tom didn't hear her feet moving against the sound-absorbing plush carpet, but he heard the quiet click of the door and he knew she'd gone. His trembling hands found the doorhandle to the balcony and he hauled the door open. Once outside he let out an almighty roar—one that was filled with anger, pain and frustration, and he let the winter breeze take it away and dump it out over the harbour.

Breathing heavily, he tried to find some calm. The

last person he'd ever expected to ring his doorbell was Hayley. Hayley, who'd felt as soft and as warm as a kitten but whose voice had told another story—the story that promised tangled sheets, sweaty bodies and the bliss of ultimate release.

He'd sensed the change between them, hell, he'd smelled it on her, and heard it in her voice after he'd accidentally pressed his hands to her breasts. Her soft, round breasts that had felt so glorious in his hands. It had been a clear invitation from her to explore and to see what might happen—a man's perfect fantasy and he'd kicked her to the kerb.

He slammed his hand hard against the metal railing, trying to silence the itch that had pleaded with him to touch her again, but the impact of the blow didn't affect it. Neither did it cool his body, which burned to feel hers moulding to his. No, all it had achieved was to make him want to kiss her even more and taste the scent of her. That potent scent he'd been inhaling from the moment she'd walked in, the interplay of sweat and desire, culminating in a powerful aphrodisiac that had made him hard and ready to lose himself in her.

But he'd also smelled sweetness and that scared him because it was a sweetness unsullied by the bastard that was fate. The bastard that had stolen his sight and continued to mock him.

He pulled his phone out of his pocket and said, 'Jared,' to activate the call, before pressing it against his ear.

'Hey, Tom.' Jared's voice sounded muffled due to the hands-free device. 'I'm pulling in now. I just saw that doctor you met the other day, only this time she was smokin' in Lycra. She's got one hot body, dude.'

'Lycra he'd just had his hands all over. One nipped-in

waist he'd cupped, and soft, soft skin he'd longed to explore. Skin he couldn't explore. Damn, he'd wanted her.

She offered you friendship.

The tempting thought tried to settle but he shrugged it away. There was no point. His life had changed the moment his brain had been jolted violently on its axis and dinner the other night had left him in no doubt that being with Hayley only reminded him of everything he'd lost. That's why he'd hurt her feelings and sent her away. He couldn't risk her coming back.

It was all about survival, pure and simple.

His survival.

He thought about the lecture hall full of medical students waiting for him, and waiting for him to make a mistake. How long would it take before they considered his experience passé?

'Tom, do you want me to come up?'

'No, stay there, Jared. I'm coming straight down.'

He picked up his computer and his cane, patted his pocket for his wallet and keys and opened the door. He paused for a moment, visualising the route: thirteen steps to the lift and avoid the ornamental palm in the unforgiving ceramic pot at step nine.

Yes, it was all about survival.

CHAPTER FIVE

'HAYLEY, come talk to us.' Theo winked and patted the space on the couch next to him. 'Been having any more dinners with dark-haired doctors?'

All the other night-duty nurses' heads turned toward her so fast she could hear cervical vertebrae cracking. Damn it, why had she asked Theo about Tom?

'I know it won't be Finn Kennedy.' Jenny looked up from her cross-stitch, sympathy in her eyes. 'I see you're back on the night-duty roster again. That's his way of saying, "Behave and don't usurp your superiors."'

Thank you, Jenny, for moving the conversation away from Tom and thank you, Mr Kennedy, for a week of nights and seven days of sleep. 'I promise I'll be well-behaved from now on.'

'Good.' Theo pulled a green badge from his pocket and handed it to her.

She stared at the picture of a light bulb with a red line through it. 'What's this?

'It's to remind you to turn out the lights. You're my worst offender. Do you realise everywhere you go you leave a trail of light behind you and that's adding to global warming? Meanwhile, ICU is whipping us and I want to win the sustainability grant. Everyone…' he paused and glared at all the staff '…has to get on board. If you're not in a room, turn out the lights.'

'I didn't realise you had a scary side, Theo.' Hayley forced a smile and stuck the badge on her scrubs, knowing that was the easy part. Turning lights off went against years of ingrained behaviour, years of using light as a refuge from fear.

'And now back to who you're dating.' Suzy Carpenter's mouth was a hard, tight line.

'Don't stress, Suzy,' Theo teased. 'There's no new doctor on the block so she's not stealing anyone from you.'

Thankfully, Hayley's pager started beeping because, short of torture, she refused to tell anyone how she'd made a fool of herself with Tom. As she read the page she quickly rose to her feet. 'This can't be good. Evie wants me downstairs stat for a consult. Gear up, gang, we could be operating soon.'

Hayley took the fire-escape stairs two at a time rather than waiting for a lift, and a couple of minutes later she was in the frantic emergency department. Nurses were speed-walking, doctors looked harried and she glimpsed three ambulances standing in the bay. It all pointed to a line-up of serious cases.

'Hayley!' Evie gave her an urgent wave while she instructed a nurse to get more dexamethasone. 'We've got a problem.' She tugged her over to a light box where a CT scan was firmly clipped. She tapped the centre of the film. 'Gretel Darlington, a nineteen-year-old woman presenting with a two-month history of vague headaches, but tonight she's had a sudden onset of severe, migraine-type headache. She's in a lot of pain, slightly disorientated, and on examination has shocking nystagmus. She's not got control over her eye movements at all.'

Hayley frowned as she stared at the black and white

image of the patient's brain, wondering exactly why Evie was showing it to her. 'She hasn't got a migraine. That tumour's the size of an orange.'

Evie moved her pen around the perimeter of the tumour. 'And she's bleeding. She needs surgery now to relieve the pressure.'

'Absolutely.' Hayley had no argument with the diagnosis or the treatment plan, but she was totally confused as to why Evie had paged her. 'Exactly what's this case got to do with me?'

The usually unflappable Evie had two deep lines carved into her forehead and her hazel eyes radiated deep concern. 'You have to do the surgery.'

Tingling shock whooshed through Hayley so fast she gaped. 'I'm a general surgical registrar, Evie, and this girl needs a neurosurgeon!'

'You think I don't know that?' Evie shoved her hair behind her ears with an air of desperation. 'Rupert Davidson is at a conference with his registrar and Lewis Renwick, the on-call neurosurgeon, is already in surgery over at RPH. By the time he finishes there and drives over the bridge to here, it could be three hours or more. She doesn't have that much time.'

Hayley bit her lip. 'There *has* to be a neurosurgeon in private practice we can call.'

'Tried that. The problem is that most of Sydney's neurosurgeons are at the Neurosurgical Society of Australasia's conference.' She shrugged, the action full of resignation. 'It's in Fiji this year and because it's winter more than the usual number went, leaving all the hospitals stretched.'

'What about Finn Kennedy? He's got all that trauma experience from his time in the army.'

Evie flinched. 'He's not answering his pages. It's you, Hayley.'

Brain surgery. A million thoughts tore around her mind driven by fear and ranging from whether she could actually do the surgery without damaging the patient to possible law suits against her. She was in Sydney, NSW, not Africa. This lack of appropriate surgeons shouldn't have happened here and yet circumstances had contrived to put her in this position. To put her patient in this position.

She stared at the scan again, but it didn't change the picture. The brain fitted snugly inside the bony protection of the skull and the design didn't allow for anything else. No extra fluid, no blood, no extra growths. Nothing.

She was between a rock and a hard place. If she didn't operate, the woman would die. If she did operate, she risked the life of her patient and her career. She could just see and hear the headlines of the tabloid papers and the sensational television current affairs programmes if something went wrong.

'Evie, it's so damn risky, and not just for the patient.'

The ER doctor's hand gripped her shoulder. 'Believe me, if there was another option, I would have taken it. Pretend we're in Darwin, Hayley. All emergency neurosurgery up there is done by general surgeons.'

She shook her head. 'That doesn't reassure me.'

The scream of sirens outside muted as Hayley forced herself to block out everything except the task at hand. Slowly the chaos that Evie's request had generated started to fade and her thoughts lined up in neat rows—problem, options for best outcome, solution.

Tom.

The thought steadied her. There was a neurosurgeon close by. Now wasn't the time to think about what had happened the last time they'd met. About his completely unambiguous rejection of her. This was a medical emergency and the stakes were life and death. All personal feelings got set aside. Must be set aside no matter how hard.

'Evie, go grab a taxi and send it to the Bridgeview Building.' She grabbed the phone on the wall and punched 9 for the switchboard. 'It's Hayley Grey. Connect me to Mr Tom Jordan, now. It's an emergency.'

The shrill ring of the phone on Tom's bedside table woke him with a jerk. Once he'd always slept lightly, used to being woken at all hours by the hospital, but two years on from the last time he'd worked as a surgeon and his body clock had changed. Now the only thing that woke him at three a.m. was his own thoughts.

Completely out of practice, he shot out his hand and immediately knocked into the lamp. He heard the crash and swore before reaching the phone. Hell, this had better not be a wrong number or he'd just sacrificed a lamp for nothing. Not that he technically needed it. Hating not being able to read caller ID, and not recognising the ringtone, he grunted down the phone. 'Tom Jordan.'

'Tom, it's Hayley.'

This time he instantly recognised her sultry voice and his gut rolled on a shot of desire so pure that it couldn't be mistaken for anything else. He immediately chased it away with steely determination. The sort of single-mindedness that had driven him to become the youngest head of neurosurgery, and now drove him to master braille and attempt echolocation so he could be as independent as possible. He wouldn't allow himself to want Hayley. It would only make him weak.

She wanted you. He sighed at the memory and now it was the middle of the night and a week since he'd been beyond rude to her to keep her away from him. Was this a drunken booty call or a drunken 'how dare you reject me?' call? Either way, he didn't need it. He ran his free hand through his hair. 'Hayley, don't say anything you're going to regret in the light of day.'

'I need you, Tom.'

And she'd just gone and said it. 'Look, Hayley, I tried to make it clear the other day that—'

'This is *nothing* to do with the other day.' The cutting tone in her voice could have sliced through rope. 'Just listen to me. There's a young woman in ER with a brain tumour and an associated bleed. There isn't a neurosurgeon available between here and Wollongong and I have to operate. Now. I need you in Theatre with me, Tom. I need you to talk me through it. Be my guide.'

He heard the fear in her voice and it matched his own. There was a huge difference between being able to see the operating field whilst guiding a registrar through the procedure and depending on Hayley telling him what she was seeing so he could tell her what to do next. 'Can dexamethasone reduce the swelling enough to hold her until the guy from Wollongong arrives?'

'No.' Her tone softened slightly. 'Believe me, Tom, if I had any other choice I would have taken it but there isn't one. We are this girl's only chance.'

He swung his legs over the side of the bed. 'Hell, she's having a really bad day, then.'

'She is.' Hayley's strained laugh—the one all medical personnel used when things were at their darkest—vibrated down the line, bringing with it a camaraderie that called out to him.

'I've sent a taxi, which is probably arriving any minute. I'll see you at the scrub sinks, Tom.'

The line went dead.

The scrub sinks.

She'd rung off, leaving him with no option.

He was going back to Operating Room One. Going home. Only home was supposed to be a place of sanctuary and safety and this felt like walking off a cliff.

'You didn't shave off all her hair, did you?'

Tom sat on a stool behind Hayley, noticing the varied array of smells in the operating room that he'd never noticed when he'd been sighted. Disinfectant mixed in with anaesthetic gases and blood, plus a couple of other aromas he couldn't quite identify and wasn't certain he wanted to. But no matter how pungent the odours, Hayley's perfume floated on top of them all in a combination of freshness, sunshine and summer flowers. He wanted to breathe in more deeply.

'No, we only shaved off half her ponytail.'

'Good. Neurosurgery is a huge invasion and I always make it a point to shave the bare minimum out of respect for the patient.'

Made it a point. You're not operating any more.

Being back here felt surreal—he was in his theatre that wasn't his any more, part of a team rather than leading it. He wasn't scrubbed. Hell, he couldn't remember the last time he'd been in the OR and not scrubbed. Probably when he'd been a med student. He interlocked his fingers, keeping his hands tightly clasped together in his lap.

He heard Hayley murmuring to the anaesthetist and then she said, 'Tom, I have Theo scrubbed in, David's the anaesthetist, Jenny is scouting and Suzy—' she seemed to hit the name with an edge '—is assisting David.'

He and Suzy had shared a fun night three years ago after one of the OR dinners, but he'd never called her. He'd never called any woman because work and patients had always come first and he would never allow anyone to derail him from his goal of staying on top and keeping the demons of his childhood at bay.

He could feel the gaze of many on him and then came the chorus of 'Hello, Tom', just as it had when he'd owned this space and had been called in for a night-time emergency. He knew everyone and he also knew, despite all their idiosyncrasies, they worked together as a team. Given the circumstances, Hayley had the best support she could have.

'Tom, the pinion's in place, holding Gretel's head in position, so let's start.'

To someone who'd not met her before, Hayley's voice would have sounded confident, but Tom detected her massive stress levels in the tiny alto quavers. She'd explained the scan to him earlier and he could picture it all very clearly in his mind. 'Due to the position of the mass, you're making a lateral incision and then performing a suboccipital craniotomy.'

'Removing a bone flap to relieve the pressure,' Hayley muttered as if it was a mantra. 'That's the easy part.'

It is. 'One step at a time and we'll get through this.' But he too was talking out loud to reassure himself as much as everyone else. So much could go wrong in so many unpredictable ways and he couldn't see a damn thing.

He'd always operated with music playing, but not soothing classical. His OR would vibrate with hard rock and, during extremely tense moments, heavy metal. Hayley was operating in silence so he sat listening to the whoosh of the respirator and the hiss of the suction, which only ramped up his agitation. He started to hum.

'Tom, I've turned the skin flap and I can see bone.'

'Now you use the high-speed drill and make three small burr holes into the skull.'

The shrill shriek of the drill against bone always made

medical and nursing students jump the first time they heard it. Tom had always teased and laughed at their reaction, but he didn't laugh today. Instead, his fingers clenched against nothing, wishing they were holding the drill, wishing he was able to do the job, not just for himself but for the patient. *For Hayley.*

The shriek died away. 'Done.' Hayley swallowed. 'What's next?'

He visualised the silver instruments all laid out in neat rows on the green sterile sheet. 'Use the Midas Rex drill to create the bone flap.'

'Oh, my, it's like a can opener.' Hayley gave a tight laugh and a few moments later said, 'The bone flap's removed and I can see the dura.'

Like an illustrated textbook, Tom's mind beamed the image Hayley was looking at. 'Excellent. Now you need the grooved director. It's your atraumtic guide. Using the scalpel, cut the dura over the groove and this protects the brain tissue underneath.'

'Too easy.'

But the everyday slang expression was laden with her anxieties. He moved to reassure her. 'You're doing fine, Hayley. David, how's our patient?'

'She's holding her own at the moment, but I'll be happier when Hayley's stopped the bleeding.'

'You're not alone there.' Tom counted to ten because he didn't want to rush Hayley, but he also needed to keep her within a particular time frame. 'Can you see brain tissue, Hayley?'

'I've found the clot.' Her relief filled the theatre.

'Theo, position the microscope.'

The rustle of plastic-covered equipment being wheeled into place was the only sound and Tom hated not being able to see what was going on. 'Hurry up, Theo.'

'It's in position now, Tom,' Theo said.

'Good. Hayley, have you found the bleeding?'

'Give me a minute, I'm still looking.'

Her normally mellow voice rose as her semblance of calm shredded at the edges. Tom wished he could take over, relieve her of this unwanted task that was stretching her and forcing her to go places she'd never been before. But he was powerless to help so he did the next best thing. 'Theo, suction the clot and keep the field clear. She needs to be able to see.'

'On it, Tom,' the nurse replied.

For a moment all he could hear was the gurgle of suction and he couldn't stop his foot from tapping on the floor.

'Okay.' Hayley's breath came out in a rush. 'I see it.'

Thank you. 'Stop the bleeding with the bipolar forceps.'

'What if that doesn't work?'

Don't panic on me now, Hayley. He infused his voice with a calm he didn't feel. This surgery was something he'd perfected over years of training. Hayley was being thrown in feet first. 'We've got the option of clipping, but try the electrical coagulation first because it will probably work.'

Please let it work. The sooner she stopped the bleeding, the better it was for their patient.

He held his breath while Hayley worked, but he could only guess at what was going on because, apart from a few muttered words, she was silent. He'd always grunted, yelled, talked and even sung his way through surgery. Her silence was unnerving.

'Suction, Theo,' Hayley snapped.

'Her intracranial pressure's still rising.' David sounded seriously worried.

'Has it worked?' Tom hoped like hell it had.

'Pray that it has,' Hayley said. 'This is the moment of truth, team.'

No one said a word. Only the buzz and whirr of the machines dared to make a sound as time slowed down, stretching out interminably and reaching into infinity.

'Yes!' Hayley's woot of relief bounced around him. 'Field is clear. Bleeding's stopped. Clot's evacuated. We did it. Thank goodness I'm sitting down or my legs would collapse.'

'Great job. You've done well.' Tom grinned, wanting to high-five her. She'd held her nerve in a tight corner and now step one was complete. He immediately focused. 'Don't get too excited. You've stopped the bleeding, but we've still got the problem of the pressure. With a mass that size you're going to have to excise a part of it so the brain can get some relief and relax. This takes the risk of her brain herniating down to zero. We also need a biopsy for pathology so we can hand over to Lewis Renwick, who'll operate to remove the rest of the tumour in a day or so.'

'You make it all sound so simple.'

'It's just brain surgery.'

Like a pressure valve being released, everyone laughed. Despite the life-threatening emergency, the fraught conditions and the fact he couldn't operate, something inside Tom relaxed. Something that hadn't relaxed in a very, very long time.

Hayley felt utterly shattered as she walked toward ICU. Even though it had only been three and a half hours since she'd operated on Gretel, it felt like years ago. Having used up every ounce of her concentration whilst operating on her neurological patient, she'd expected to be able to fall in a quivering heap the moment the surgery was over.

Instead, just as Tom and David had left the OR to escort Gretel to ICU, she'd been called back down to Emergency for another consultation. Half an hour later she'd been scrubbed again and busy resecting an ischaemic bowel. It hadn't been an easy operation either.

Now pink streaks of dawn clung to the clouds and all she wanted was her bed, but she couldn't go home without calling in to see Gretel. She pushed open the doors, checked the patient board, and walked directly to cubicle four. She stood at the end of the ICU bed and blinked. Twice. Shooting out her hand, she gripped the edge of the bed as her legs threatened to collapse in shock. She didn't know what stunned her more, the fact that Gretel—whose head she'd had her hands inside a few short hours ago— was sitting up, awake and talking to two doctors, or that Tom was one of those doctors.

He was sitting by the bed, holding Gretel's hand. His face had lost its taut expression—the one she'd become convinced was a permanent part of him—and he looked almost happy.

Tom turned slowly and his nostrils flared. 'Hayley?'

A buzz of hope streaked along her veins. *He knows it's you.*

It's not personal. He's got ninja olfactory skills.

She nodded automatically and then realised her mistake. 'Yes, Tom, it's me.'

'Lewis…' Tom threw his arm out toward her '…meet Hayley Grey, the registrar who operated on Gretel.'

A man in a crumpled suit extended his hand in greeting along with a tired smile. 'Lewis Renwick. Last neurosurgeon in Sydney, it seems. Sorry I was tied up at RPH, but Tom's been telling me that you coped admirably. Looking at the most recent scan, I agree. You've done a wonderful job.'

Hayley grinned with relief. 'Thank you, but I'm pretty good at following instructions.'

Lewis laughed. 'Which is fortunate as Tom's pretty good at giving them.'

Tom's dark brows rose but a grin clung to his lips. 'Only because most people need them.'

Gretel smiled and touched her hair. 'Thanks, Dr Grey, not just for saving my life but for saving most of my hair.'

'You're very welcome, but it was very much a team event, with Mr Jordan guiding me through it.'

'I know, he told me all about it.' Gretel glanced between the three of them, but spoke directly to Hayley. 'I can't believe all this has happened to me, but at least the tumour isn't cancerous. I'm so lucky that you and Mr Jordan were here tonight and now to have Mr Renwick looking after me.'

Tom patted Gretel's hand and gave her a big wink. 'He's almost as good a neurosurgeon as me except for his lousy taste in music.'

'So now you're taking on Mozart?' Lewis folded his arms in mock effrontery.

'I always let my patients choose their playlist for the awake part of their surgery.'

The joking faded from Tom's voice and Hayley saw how much he missed hospital life. It wasn't just the surgery but his patients as well. Perhaps the patients even more than the surgery? The thought hovered for a moment before she discarded it.

'I tell you what, Gretel…' Lewis made a note on her chart '…ask your family to bring in your MP3 player and as long as there's no hip-hop on it, you can listen to your music while I'm removing the tumour and the anaesthetist is asking you questions.'

'That's awesome, Mr Renwick. Thank you.' Gretel

touched the bandage on her head. 'It's going to be weird being awake while you're operating on my brain.'

Hayley gave Gretel's foot a pat. 'I'll leave you to talk to Mr Renwick about the surgery as I'm heading home now, but I'll call by later tonight when I'm back on duty.'

'I'll come with you.' Tom rose and flicked out his cane.

Hayley's feet stayed still in surprise. He'd been brilliant in Theatre, but she could still vividly remember what he'd said when he'd first answered the phone. Now he wanted to leave with her? It didn't make sense.

He's in ICU with machines everywhere. He'll need some guidance to get to the safety of the corridor.

Yep, that would be it.

Logic didn't stop the sneaking fizz of disappointment.

'You're in good hands, Gretel.' Tom's voice suddenly took on a parental tone with an underlying warning. 'Take care of her, Lewis.'

Hayley stepped up to Tom and said quietly, 'Would you like to put your hand on my shoulder or tap your way out?'

His entire body stiffened. 'I'll take your elbow.'

She lifted his hand and guided it to her left elbow. 'Are you ready?'

'As I'll ever be.'

The prickly man was back and she didn't try to make polite conversation. She walked normally, but she did slow just before the nurses' station. 'Do you want to speak to any staff before you leave?'

He frowned and his mouth flattened. 'Is there any point? Gretel isn't my patient.'

She didn't even try to stop the snarky tone in her voice. 'Oh, right. How could I have possibly forgotten that you don't do social niceties?'

The corner of his mouth twitched, but he didn't say a word.

She kept walking and was about to say 'The door is just ahead' when Tom got in first.

'Five steps to the door,' he said. 'If you open it, I'll walk through the doorway and meet you on the other side.'

'Okay.' She did as he asked and then rejoined him in the corridor. She wondered if he might insist on walking on his own but he took her arm again.

As the music played around them in the lift, he said, 'You did a great job today.'

'Thank you.' The ping sounded and the doors opened.

He gave a brisk nod. 'I'm going to use the exit into the lane.'

She thought about where she'd run the other day. 'The one where Pete's got the rubbish dumpster?'

'That's it.'

It was on the other side of the hospital from the exit she usually used, and she wondered if it was Tom code for *I'll walk on my own now*? But he hadn't let go of her arm so she kept walking with him toward the door. Just as Hayley pushed open the heavy external door, a ward clerk, hurrying in for the morning shift, stopped to let them through.

'Mr Jordan?' The woman's face lit up with a huge smile. 'It's Penny. It's so great to see you. You've been missed.'

Tom extended his hand, which the clerk pressed warmly. 'Penny, it's great to hear your voice. How's Ben doing?'

'He's thriving, thanks to you. Can you believe that he's even playing football in the under nines?'

Tom moved his head toward her voice. 'I can believe it. He was a determined kid and I'm pleased to know he's doing so well.' He gave her a warm smile. 'You take care, Penny.'

Hayley stared at him, hardly able to recognise the man standing next to her.

Be fair. He was like this with Gretel.

Just not with me. Her silent sigh dragged her shoulders down a touch.

'You take care too, Mr Jordan.' Penny squeezed Tom's hand again. 'Goodbye.' She hurried inside to work and the door slammed shut behind her.

Tom's grip on Hayley's arm increased ever so slightly and he leaned in towards her, his deep voice caressing her ear and sparking such a swirl of longing that she wanted to move her head so her lips would brush his.

'And you thought I didn't do social chitchat.' He tapped his cane and grinned. 'Time to pick your jaw up off the ground, Hayley Grey.'

Just when she thought she'd got Tom Jordan figured out, he went and did something totally unpredictable like this. She tried to close her gaping mouth, but before she could, a giggle escaped, and then another and another, until she couldn't stop. It was like her veins were full of laughter bubbles and they just kept rising to the surface, being carried up on a wave of fatigue and sheer relief that the night was finally over. Everything seemed uproariously funny and she gave in to it, loving the reckless feeling and the joy that came with it.

Tom's bass laugh joined hers, making her laugh even harder until tears streamed down her face, her sides ached and she could hardly hold her head up. She let it fall onto his shoulder as she gasped for breath. 'I don't even know why I'm laughing.'

'The non-technical term is slap happy.' He pressed his

free hand gently against her hair. 'It's a release for the pressure of the last few hours.'

She raised her head, loving the way his hand now curved around the back of her neck. 'It doesn't usually happen to me.'

'You don't usually do brain surgery.' Now his fingers were stroking her neck and then they moved along her jaw, tilting her chin. His eyes that couldn't see her darkened with desire. 'You were amazing. Are amazing.'

Her laughter faded at his voice—husky, filled with admiration and undisguised attraction. Unlike the last time they'd almost kissed, this time there was no ambiguity. This time his words and tone of voice matched his expression. Nothing about him was pushing her away.

Her brain melted into a puddle of need as he traced her mouth with the tips of his fingers. Zips of sensation tore through her, detonating heat, lust and a desperate yearning all over her body. Then his mouth pressed against hers— gentle yet firm and, oh, so scorching hot. She heard a soft moan as she opened her mouth under his and realised it had come from her. His taste flooded her—coffee, peppermint and hunger for her—swirling into her mouth, diving deep and strumming the strings of her need. It knocked her off her feet.

She sagged against him. He stumbled slightly at the unexpected weight and she flung her arm around his waist to steady him. She didn't want to give him any reason to pull away. She closed her eyes and let him kiss her, giving him full rein to explore her mouth, to nip her lips with his teeth, to caress and explore with his tongue and to brand her with his flavour of arousal. Sinking into the kiss, his heat simmered her blood, making every pulse point throb, and she never wanted it to end.

She'd been kissed before but nothing like this. It was

as if he was stealing part of her and she was giving it up freely, but still he demanded more and she could feel the pull. Suddenly her blissed-out body woke up and demanded him. She cupped his cheeks, felt his stubble grazing her palms and she kissed him back.

Hard.

Fast.

Her tongue duelled with his and dominated his mouth, seeking his fire and merging it with hers. She heard him moan, heard his cane fall to the ground and felt his mouth plunder hers with a weight that stole her breath.

Panting, he tore his mouth away from hers and she shivered from the loss of his touch.

His hand ploughed through his hair. 'Hell, I used to have a lot more finesse than this. We're standing next to a rubbish dumpster.'

'I hadn't noticed.' She touched his cheek, wanting to keep the contact. Not wanting him to change his mind.

He laughed and brought his hand up to cover hers. 'Your sense of smell is hopeless.'

'I thought we were dealing with a whole lot of other senses and, believe me, you still have loads of finesse.' She kissed him quickly and decided to act. 'I don't have my car, but my place isn't far. It's over on Northcliff.'

He smiled and his eyes seemed to sparkle like the phosphorescent green waters of the Great Barrier Reef. 'Mine's closer. Walk fast.'

CHAPTER SIX

Tom stretched out in his bed, feeling completely sated. The musky smell of sex, the sweet scent of Hayley and the warmth from her body circled him, and he realised he hadn't felt this relaxed since— Hell, he had no clue how long it had been and at that moment he didn't care. He just was. He grinned at the play of light and dark in the room, shadows cast by the morning light. They'd made it to his apartment—just. Somehow he'd got his trembling hand to insert the key into the lock and had managed to turn it and open the door. In a tumble of clothes, they'd kicked off shoes, popped buttons, got arms tangled up in sleeves and shucked pants until finally they'd fallen into his bed and come together in a rush of blood-pounding desire and screaming lust—hot, fast and breath-stealing. Nothing about it had been slow. Nothing about it had been measured. It had been all about need—his and hers—two people equal in their quest to lose themselves in each other, taking more than giving.

Now, as his lungs refilled with air and his blood came back to his brain, the full impact of what had just happened hit him. He had a woman in *his* bed. A woman in his apartment. Before he'd gone blind, he'd always had sex with a woman at her place. That way he had been the one in control. He could get up and leave when he was ready, sometimes before he was ready if the hospital called him out—but either way his departure took place prior to the woman snuggling up and falling asleep on his shoulder. He'd always mumble something about 'work' and 'calling later', which, of course, he never did. Work had always come first because it protected him from tumbling back to poverty and the griminess of his childhood.

The mattress moved and he reached his hand out to touch Hayley's silky hair, surprised at the need he had to feel her presence.

You never went in for touchy-feely stuff.

The last time I had sex I wasn't blind. This is my way of seeing her.

If you say so.

He blocked out his internal argument. 'You okay, Hayley?'

'I'm fine. Why?'

He heard the smile in her voice. 'It was pretty fast.'

She gave a throaty laugh. 'Fast, but good, I hope.'

'Very good.' And it had been. Intoxicatingly good, and his blood still sang with her taste and touch. The buzz reminded him of the high he'd always got from riding his 1000 cc motorcycle fast along the coast with the throb of the powerful engine vibrating through him, and the wind and salt pounding him. It was amplified exhilaration and totally addictive. But as much as he'd loved the speed of his motorcycle and his sports car, he'd also enjoyed long, leisurely walks. That had given him a totally different buzz and that was the one he wanted now. He knew the urgent feel of Hayley's arms and legs around him, the hot press of her body against his, and her gasps of breath as she begged for him. This time he wanted to feel and hear her shatter from a long, slow build-up. From a seduction so unhurried in its approach that it would sneak up unannounced and render her deliciously helpless with its power. And then he'd join her.

Hayley felt Tom's fingers in her hair and the unhurried way they explored its length until they reached her scalp and traced the width of her forehead. The touch was gentle as opposed to urgent, which was how it had been from the moment they'd stumbled into his apartment. How she'd managed to stand next to him in the hall, watching him miss the door lock three times without lunging for the key and ripping it out of his hand and slamming it into the lock, still amazed her. Both of them had been crazy with lust and had given themselves over to it completely. Now the exhilaration was fading and exhaustion from her huge night at The Harbour was sending out its cloying tendrils. His fingers soothed and her eyes fluttered shut.

'What happened here?'

Her eyes flew open as she felt his fingers on her hairline, caressing the small scar that nestled there, hidden under her hair. No one ever saw it and yet Tom, who couldn't see, had found it. She looked up at him as he stared down at her through beautiful yet sightless eyes, knowing she was only a shadow to him. 'I fell off my bike when I was nine.'

He nodded slowly as if he was compiling a picture of her. 'What colour's your hair?'

'I say it's brown but my hairdresser insists it's chestnut. However, we both agree that it's dead straight.'

His mouth tweaked up in a half-smile. 'That I knew. Not one single curl snagged my fingers.' He breathed deeply as he ran strands of her hair across his face. 'It smells like lime and coconut.'

Her short laugh showed her embarrassment. 'I have a bit of a thing for body lotions, perfumes and shampoo, but I also know that often patients are scared before surgery so I think I should smell nice for them.'

He pressed his lips to her forehead. 'I appreciate it.'

A silly quiver of happiness shoved her embarrassment away.

His palms cupped her cheeks and his thumbs met at the bridge of her nose. He stroked outwards with a delicious amount of pressure—not firm but not soft either—and she let his touch roll over her, stripping her muscles of all their tension as she sank into the mattress. She'd never been touched quite like this. It was an almost reverent exploration that put sighted lovers in the shade. His hands brushed her eyebrows and then outlined her closed eyes.

Again Tom's voice called her back. 'Are they chestnut too?'

She struggled to concentrate as his fingers sent rivers of relaxation washing through her. 'What?'

'Your eyebrows. Are they chestnut?'

It seemed odd to be describing herself—almost vain—but she'd enjoyed watching Tom and studying him over the last ten days and this was his turn. 'No, they're darker and so are my eyelashes. With my brown eyes and long brown lashes my sister used to—' She bit off the words. She didn't want to think about Amy right now. This wasn't the real world with all its pain and heartache. This was pure escapism.

'Call you a Jersey cow?'

She gasped in surprise. 'How did you know?'

He grinned. 'Big brown eyes and long, thick lashes. It doesn't take a rocket scientist to work that one out.'

His thumbs continued to explore her face. 'Your nose is cuter than a Jersey cow's.'

'Gee, thanks.' She laughed half-indignantly and then

reached out her hand, running it along the length of his very distinctive nose and lingering on the slight bump. 'Mine hasn't been broken.'

'You probably grew up on the Northern Beaches.' It was said without rancour, but it inferred that her childhood had been easier than his.

She didn't confirm her middle-class upbringing because she knew more than anyone that money didn't protect a child from death or a family from loss. Instead, she let him capture her hand from his nose, place it by her side and then kiss her.

Deep beyond her tiredness, her body stirred.

The length of his body edged hers lightly, moving against it and then away with each breath he took. His hands brushed her chin and her neck, and then he stroked her collarbone with a feather-soft touch, lingering on the slightly raised area on the right-hand side. 'The bike accident?'

A delicious tingle spread around her body, demolishing the fatigue and waking her up in the most wonderful way. 'Who knew my body was a road map of my life? There's an appendix scar further down.'

'Poor Hayley.'

He kissed the spot where the bone had knitted, his tongue caressing her skin, and her legs twitched as the shimmers joined together into one wide river of glorious sensation. Then his hands reached her breasts and his touch became almost reverent. Cupping them, he took their weight and a deep line of concentration carved into his brow.

She was instantly self-conscious, wondering what was wrong with her breasts. 'What?'

'They're just as I imagined.'

She didn't understand. 'But you've touched them before.'

He smiled a knowing smile. 'That was a mere brush of the hand, which to a blind man is nothing more than a passing glance. Now, this…' his thumb stroked her nipple '…is really seeing them.'

A hot arrow of longing darted straight down between her legs and her body jerked against his.

This time he grinned widely. 'If you like that, you might just enjoy this.'

His mouth closed around the areola of her other breast while his thumb continued to brush the nipple. Her breasts tightened and her nipples puckered, desperately seeking more. Her breath hitched in her throat as showers of colour and ribbons of heat followed, making her head thrash against the pillow. She never wanted it to stop and her hands plunged into his hair in a combination of wanting to touch him and not wanting him to stop what he was doing.

His wicked laugh rained down on her as he dawdled his tongue and his hands down her belly, stroking her, tasting her and branding her with his stubble until her body was quivering and slick with throbbing need for him.

Her arms flailed out toward the bedside table and she managed to gasp, 'Condoms.'

He shook his head as his fingers reached the only thatch of hair on her body that was curly. 'We're not ready for that just yet.'

She stared at his face as she tried hard to bring her eyes into focus. 'We're…not?'

'No.' His fingers sneaked slowly lower and lower with blissful intent, and then he slid one inside her. Then another.

She gasped with delight and instantly tightened around

his fingers before closing her eyes and joining the ride to oblivion. Nothing existed except the ever-increasing ball of sensation that he was building inside her with his talented hands.

Suddenly, his fingers stopped and then withdrew.

Shocked surprise and begging need snapped her eyes open, fast. 'Don't stop.' She heard the desperation in her voice and didn't care. 'Please, don't stop.'

His face was wreathed in one enormous smile that crinkled the edges of his eyes, which now glowed with a light she'd never seen before. With his other hand he drew a lazy circle on her lower belly. 'Just tell me, what's the colour of the hair down here?'

She heard words, but her completely melted brain frantically scrambled, trying to find some neurons that would still connect. It tried, but the colour eluded her. 'You're a shocking tease, Tom Jordan. Does it even matter?'

'Yes. It completes my picture of you.'

The tenderness in his words touched her and the permanent emptiness around her heart shrank a little. She pressed her hand against his chest and the almost black hair that rested there. 'This colour.'

'Beautiful.'

He moved and she felt his hair lightly brush her belly and then his lips pressing kisses on her inner thigh before finding the perfect place.

Deep within, her scream of need ignited and she cried out for him, wanting him to fill her, aching for his width, but then her body took over, riding the pounding waves of wonder, sweeping her higher and higher until the ball of bliss exploded, flinging her far beyond herself to a place she'd never been.

When she floated back to earth, she pulled his face to

hers and kissed him. 'Thank you. Now I want to give you the same gift.'

'And you can.'

He rolled her over so he was under her and then he pressed a foil square into her hand. She rolled the condom over his erection, marvelling at his long, silky length, and she kept stroking him, loving the feel of him against her palm.

He groaned and his face flushed. 'Listening to you come almost undid me so if you want the full experience you need to stop doing that right now.'

'Really?' She leaned forward, letting her hair sweep across his chest, surprised but loving the fact that her orgasm had turned him on when she'd seen it as a selfless gift from him.

He grabbed her buttocks and lifted her. 'Believe me. Really.'

A surge of power filled her—her femininity rising to dominate for the very first time in her life. This sightless man desired her and wanted her, and just as he'd held the key to demolishing all her restraint, she now held the key to his. She also knew that by giving him release she too would receive it. Lowering her body slowly, she felt herself opening up layer upon layer to take him, to absorb him, and then she closed tightly around him.

His guttural groan filled the room and then his hands gripped her hips. In a rhythm as old as time they moved together, driving each other upward, taking and giving, needing and demanding, until they both cried out with the glory of touching the stars.

Warmth cocooned Hayley. Warmth, cosiness and blissful rest. Everything around her was fuzzy—a sort of soft focus—and she had an overwhelming feeling of being safe. She didn't know how she'd come to be on a beach, lying on a large and lovely soft towel, or how long she'd even been here, but it didn't matter. She had sunshine on her back, the soporific lapping sounds of a gentle tide against the sand, and the sleep she always craved beckoned her with an addictive serenade. The Sandman with his dancing eyes said, 'Sunshine so you can sleep in a lovely pale red glow. I did this just for you. You know you want to sleep so close your eyes and leave the rest to me.'

And she was so very tired. Chronically tired from years of not getting enough sleep and this was all so perfect. She let her book fall from her hands as she laid her head down and then she let her eyelids fall shut.

The promised pink glow surrounded her and all her stress and fatigue rolled away, absorbed by the heat of the sand. The beguiling Sandman was right. This was the perfect place to sleep. Why had it taken so long to find this beach? She might never leave. As she stretched out with a sigh, the pink glow deepened to a claret-red. She fell deeper into sleep. A shiver ran along her spine as a cool breeze sneaked in around her back. She rolled over, chasing the sun, but it vanished, leaving darkness in its place. Her hand shot out, grasping for the heat of the sand, but instead of warm silica and quartz crystals she touched cold, lifeless marble. She pulled her hand back in fright as the inky darkness intensified, roaring in, settling over her like the membrane of suffocating plastic and denying her breath.

Her heart slammed against her chest as panic screamed in her ears. She gasped for breath, desperately trying to flee the dark and find the light. The more she fought the dark, the stronger its grip on her became until it pinned her down, trapping her in its clutches. She tried to stand but her legs were tied and everything she touched burned her with desolate cold.

Get out. Get out now before you die.

Panting hard, she gave an almighty push and kicked hard. Her eyes flew open and she realised she was now awake—abruptly jolted out of a nightmare. Her tight chest formed a band around her and she could hardly move any air and her head spun while her fingertips tingled.

Breathe in, breathe out. Count it in, count it out. Gradually, her eyes adjusted to the dark. Her skin was drenched in sweat, her legs felt constricted and slowly she realised she was in a bed and tangled up in a sheet and duvet. A tiny chink of light squeezed through a small gap at the closing point of the curtains.

Curtains? She never closed the curtains during the day.

And then she remembered. She was in Tom's bed.

Her arm reached out and patted cold sheets. Alone in Tom's bed.

Kicking her legs free of the rope-like sheet and pushing the duvet back, she jumped up and whipped open the curtains. Sunshine flooded the room and she fell back onto the bed and pushed herself up onto a pile of pillows. She was safe. A half laugh and half groan rumbled up from deep inside her and she automatically turned toward the bedside table, seeking a clock. But no green or red digital display greeted her. Instead, there was a large black cube with a big button on top. She pressed it and then jumped in surprise when an automated male voice said, "It's three-seventeen p.m., Wednesday, August nineteen."

She'd been asleep for seven hours? That totally stunned her. Despite the nightmare wake-up, she'd slept soundly, and in a foreign bed. She never slept very well and what sleep she was able to get always occurred in her own bed with the blinds wide open. It had been light when she'd fallen asleep and Tom must have closed the curtains for her when he'd got up, thinking it would help her sleep.

Mind-blowing sex was why you slept so well.

She grinned like a child who'd just been given a lollipop. Tom had been the most amazing lover and going by his moans and groans and panting breath she hadn't been too shoddy either. She could feel the ache of muscles that hadn't been used for a long time and just the thought of what had made them ache made her tingle.

Three o'clock. She had four hours before she had to be at work. It was time to get up and bring Tom back to bed for an hour or so before she had to head home and get ready for work. Maybe they could even grab an early dinner. Ignoring the crumpled scrubs on the floor, she whipped the sheet off the bed. Wrapping it around herself like a strapless gown, she was aiming for a seductive look—or, for Tom, a seductive feel—and she walked out into the open-plan room saying, 'Thanks for letting me sleep. I… Oh.'

The same young man she'd seen the first morning she'd met Tom was sitting at the large table in front of a laptop with a couple of textbooks open next to him. His face wore a wide grin as he stared at her, appreciating the look.

'Hello.' His blue eyes rested on her cleavage.

She gripped the top of the sheet more tightly and pulled the trailing section forward, making sure her back and legs were fully covered. Her chin shot up in an attempt to make her look a lot more in control than she felt. 'Hi. I'm Hayley.'

'Yeah, I know. Tom said.' He kept on grinning as if he'd witnessed exactly what had gone down in the bedroom seven hours earlier.

Oh, God, shoot me now. 'And you're…?'

He jumped to his feet as if her question had suddenly

woken him up and kick-started his manners. 'Jared. Jared Perkins.'

'Jared.' She took a breath to slow down her delivery and keep a handle on her embarrassment. 'Is Tom home?'

He shook his sandy-coloured head. 'No.'

'Are you expecting him back soon?'

'He's at work.' He picked up a printed piece of paper and consulted it. 'He's got an evening lecture and I'm picking him up at seven.'

'Right.' Her brain started churning over times and dates. Tom finished work at seven and she started work at seven. 'Did he leave a message?'

'No.'

Disappointment slugged her and she tried to brush it away. It wasn't like they'd made an arrangement to meet. Rational thought zoomed in, making her practical. She was standing dressed in nothing but a sheet for a man who wasn't even here. It was time to go home. She ducked back into the bedroom, dumped the sheet, pulled on her clothes and ran her fingers through her hair before snagging it back into a ponytail with a hair-tie she found in her pocket. She didn't look in the mirror because it would be far too depressing and gave up a quick wish that she didn't meet anyone she knew on the walk home, which was a sure-fire guarantee that she would.

When she returned to the living area, Jared was sitting back at the table, reading one of the textbooks. In his bright-coloured board shorts and surfing T-shirt, he looked as if he belonged more on Bondi Beach than inside, studying. Who was he? Tom's brother? Nephew? She realised she didn't know anything about Tom except he'd been a neurosurgeon and now he wasn't.

'Do you live here, Jared?'

'Nah. Wouldn't mind it, though.' He swung his arm out toward the balcony. 'It's an awesome view.'

'It is.' What exactly was his connection to Tom? 'Do you work for Tom?'

He shook his head emphatically. 'No, but I do stuff for him. Driving, shopping, anything he wants.'

She guessed Jared was in his late teens or early twenties and his broad accent and lack of social etiquette hinted at the possibility that he came from a less affluent suburb. Being on call for a taciturn blind man without any financial incentive struck her as unusual. 'That's very good of you.'

Jared's shoulders rolled back and he sat up straighter, as if she'd just offended him. 'No, it isn't. Tom's an awesome bloke and he saved my life.' The sincerity in his words put her rightfully back in her place.

She aimed for a conciliatory tone. 'Everyone at The Harbour says he was a brilliant surgeon.'

'Yeah.' He fiddled with the edge of the textbook, folding up the corner of the page.

Hayley waited for him to say more, to say exactly what operation Tom had performed on him, but he didn't elaborate and instead stuck his finger back on a line of text in the book and stared at it with a deep frown.

Okay. 'I'll leave you to it.' She walked to the door and had her hand on the handle when Jared said, 'You any good at chemistry?'

She stopped and turned to face him. 'Excuse me?'

'Chemistry.' His voice rose slightly with aggression, and his previously friendly and open face tightened. He picked up a sheaf of papers covered in red pen and waved them at her. 'The teacher says if I want to get into medicine I need an A and Tom says it's easy but it bloody isn't. You're a doctor, right? So you get chemistry.'

His blue eyes held the duelling expressions of 'I'm a macho guy' with 'I need help, Mum'. She realised it had cost him something to ask her. Just like she knew it cost Tom something every time he had to ask for help. She was struck by the similarity and she knew she couldn't ignore his request.

She walked back to the table and dropped her bag on a chair. 'Can you make coffee, Jared?'

'Yeah. Tom's got a machine.'

She smiled. 'Good. You make me a latte and I'll read what's causing you problems and see if I can help. Deal?'

Relief washed over his face. 'Deal.'

'If we grab some take-away, Jared, I can help you with that chemistry homework when we get home,' Tom offered as he fiddled with the seat-belt buckle, finally sliding it into the holder with a snap.

'Thanks, but I got it sorted. But if you're buying, I'll stay for take-away as long as it's pizza.'

'You finished the chemistry?' Tom wished his voice hadn't risen in surprise. He knew how hard Jared was working and chemistry wasn't something that came easily to him, but he had dogged determination and that often served a person better than natural ability without the drive to succeed.

'Don't sound so surprised, old man. You're not the only person good at this stuff.'

Jared's cocky tone was in stark contrast to the down-in-the-mouth voice he'd used earlier in the day when Tom had told him he could help him, but not until after work. He instinctively knew something else was now at play. 'Enough of the old man, kiddo.' He hit the word, teasing the youth back. 'So, just like that, you totally understand electrochemical series order, which five hours ago had you ready to quit school?'

'Yep.'

'Good for you.'

A moment of silence passed between them and then Jared said, 'Hayley helped.'

Hayley.

Hayley, who'd been fast asleep in his bed when he'd left his apartment. He'd left it way earlier than necessary because he hadn't wanted to be there when she woke up. Hell, he'd even invited Jared over under the guise of a fast internet connection and a quiet place to study well away from the noise of younger siblings, but the invitation had been all about Jared being in the apartment with him if Hayley woke up before he left for work. Insurance so they wouldn't be alone together again, because if they had been he didn't trust himself not to take her back to bed.

Blood pooled in his lap. Hell, just the thought of her had him wanting to retract his decision, but when he'd been sighted he'd never slept with a woman more than once. Well, not since he'd been a second-year registrar. He'd had one short-lived relationship with Karen, a radiographer, but he'd found within three months of dating that she'd had expectations of being considered first in his life, well ahead of study and his job. It had been a distraction he hadn't wanted or needed. At first putting study first had been all about fear of failure and fear of poverty, but then it had become so much more and nothing and no one had been allowed to come ahead of medicine and his plan to become a neurosurgeon. He'd owed Mick that. He'd owed Mick and Carol everything. Once he'd qualified he'd set his sights on heading his own department. Work had always come first and from the moment he and Karen had parted, he'd only ever spent one night with any woman.

The fact he'd achieved the pinnacles of surgical success and had now lost it all didn't seem enough of a reason to change his habits. Financially he was secure and the threat of poverty was long gone but, hell, he was still learning how to be blind. He didn't need any distractions from conquering the dark and living an independent and meaningful life.

'Hey, Tom, as well as being totally hot, she's an awesome teacher.'

Jared's enthusiasm for Hayley rang out loud and clear and Tom's jaw instinctively tightened. 'I'd appreciate it if you referred to her in terms of a surgeon and a teacher.'

'Sorry. I'm not gonna steal her from you, dude. I'd never do that.'

The apology in the young man's voice was unmistakeable and Tom regretted being short with him. He still wasn't totally certain why he had been. Yes, this morning had been amazing, but now it was over.

'Besides,' Jared continued, 'she's a bit old for me, but she's perfect for a bloke like you who's nearly forty.' He made the number sound ancient.

Tom gave a strangled laugh. 'I'm thirty-nine, thank you, and if you keep on about it I'll buy Chinese instead of pizza.'

'You're the same age as my dad.' The teasing had vanished from Jared's voice, leaving only regret.

Tom flinched. He hadn't meant to remind the boy of his absent father or of his tough home life. He turned toward the sound of his voice and smiled. 'I'm thinking two large La Dolce Vita specials with the lot.'

'And a garlic pizza. Order them now and make sure they throw in the gelato because last time you let them rip you off and you don't want me saying you're getting old and soft.'

Tom's mouth tweaked up into a smile. 'Just drive the damn car, Jared.'

CHAPTER SEVEN

As the tinny beat-bop music filled the operating theatre, Hayley looked up from the screen, which showed the magnified image of Mrs Papadopoulos's stone-filled gallbladder and she asked, 'Is that my phone?'

The moment the four little words were airborne, she wanted to pull the words back. She'd forgotten that Jenny wasn't scouting for this operation.

'I'll check,' said Suzy.

Dread crawled along her skin. Why did it have to be Suzy? For the first time in days Hayley willed that the phone call *not* be from Tom.

It was close to the end of a long shift—twelve midnight to twelve noon—the result of a crazy idea from someone in Administration who thought it might help diminish the surgical waiting list. It meant the team had a foot in both the night shift with its emergencies and the elective routine of the day shift morning.

'Answer it quickly, Suzy.' Theo rolled his eyes as if the sound was burning his ears. 'Hayley, of all the ringtones that state-of-the-art phone of yours has, why did you choose that one? You have to change it.'

'I can't.' She dropped her gaze back to the screen as she manoeuvred everything into position in preparation to sever the gallbladder from its anchoring stump. 'I accidentally washed my lovely phone and now it's tucked up in rice in a vague hope it might work again. Meanwhile, I've bought a temporary cheap phone and it only comes with one ringtone and one volume.'

'My ears are aching already.' With a gloved hand Theo held out a kidney dish.

Hayley dropped the badly scarred gallbladder onto the silver monometal and tried not to glance around at Suzy and ask who was calling. It had been five days since she'd seen Tom. Five days since she'd experienced the best sex of her life and then slept the most deeply she could ever remember, but since she'd left his apartment there'd been no messages, no texts, no emails, nothing. Just one long and empty silence that dragged through each day, seemingly extending it way beyond its twenty-fours.

Get over it. He never said he'd call. You never expected him to call.

Logically, she knew that they'd only acted on their simmering attraction and had come together to defuse the stress after a huge operation—that meant it had been a one-off fling. This sort of thing happened between staff occasionally, especially after a life-and-death situation. It was a type of coping mechanism—a way to share the crisis with the only other person who really understood exactly what had happened and the ramifications of how close it had come to going horribly wrong.

At least I had him.

She bit her lip as she realised with a hollow feeling that she now had something in common with Suzy. She'd used Tom and she'd let him use her. Not that she wanted to keep Tom as hers, or at least she didn't think she did, but she hated that she'd allowed herself to become a phone vulture. Twenty-four hours after leaving Tom's penthouse, she'd started circling her phone, constantly waiting for it to either ring or beep with a message, and when either of those two things happened, diving for it and hoping it was Tom. Now she'd even allowed her guard to fall and had asked out loud in front of her gossipy staff.

It's time to get a grip.

Her reaction to the whole Tom situation was totally new to her and, if she was honest, scared her just a little bit. She'd certainly never been this jumpy or spent this much time thinking about Richard or Sam. Or any other man.

'Dr Grey's phone.' Suzy's voice held the same thread of dislike that was always present when she spoke to Hayley, but never seemed to be in attendance when she spoke to the other staff. 'Oh, hello.' Warmth suddenly infused her voice. 'It's Suzy Carpenter.'

Hayley heard the change in her tone and panic made her swing around.

Suzy mouthed, 'Lachlan McQuillan.'

Relief rolled through Hayley that it wasn't Tom and she wasn't about to become the target for gossip.

Suzy continued talking to Hayley's counterpart on the other side of the surgical registrar's roster. Lach usually called Hayley for a handover just prior to starting his shift.

She let Suzy flirt with the Scot while she stitched up the four small incisions she'd made. 'David, I'm done. Thanks, everyone.' She stepped back and stripped off her gloves, leaving the nurses to clean up and the anaesthetist to extubate the patient before handing her over to the care of the recovery nurses.

Suzy was still talking to Lachlan when Hayley put out her hand out for her phone. Suzy glared at her before purring down the line, 'See you at Pete's soon.'

The nurse slapped the phone into Hayley's hand before stalking off, and Hayley rubbed her temples as she put the phone to her ear. Lachlan was just coming back after two days off so the chances of Suzy catching him at Pete's anytime soon were slim.

'Hey, Lach, it's been a quiet night, but if you can keep an eye on Mrs Papadopoulos's blood pressure for me, that would be good.'

'Not a problem, Hayley, lass. Enjoy your sleep.'

'Study more like it. I've got two days off and the exams get closer every day.'

'Aye, they do. It's a shame you missed Finn Kennedy's talk on the surgical considerations of gunshot wounds this morning. The man might be a devil to work for but he knows his stuff.'

'Have you operated with him?' Hayley hadn't told anyone what had happened in the OR with Finn because everyone was allowed a bad day, but it still niggled at her and she wanted another person's opinion.

'Aye, last week. He makes it all look so easy while the rest of us struggle just to finish the job.'

So that was it, then. She'd caught Finn Kennedy on a bad day.

Lachlan continued. 'I stayed on afterwards and caught Tom Jordan's lecture for the final-year medical students about extratemporal epilepsy.'

Tom. Her heart jumped, filling the empty space around it and she had to force herself to sound casual. 'Anything interesting?'

'Aye. Fascinating.' His Scottish accent always sounded stronger when he was excited about something. 'His patient kept spinning and experiencing memory gaps and Tom had a hunch. So, using electrodes for a month, he charted the electrical impulses and from there he removed a three-centimetre-diameter piece of brain from the seventeen-year-old. Turns out it was at the bottom of a malformation called a sulcus dysplasia and the boy's stopped spinning. Amazing stuff.'

'He gives a good lecture, that's for sure.' Worried that her voice would give her away, she switched topics. 'But listen, can you email me any notes from Kennedy's lecture, which is more our area?'

He laughed. 'Sure, although I hear you've taken to brain surgery. I'd better be careful or you'll be making me look second-class.'

'I was lucky, Lach. Believe me, you don't need the stress.'

'Aye, you're right. Enjoy your break.'

Thanks, Lach—' But he'd hung up before she could finish. She slipped her phone into her pocket and rubbed her chest, unused to it feeling this way. The fuller sensation hadn't vanished when her heart had finally resumed its normal rhythm. It was an odd feeling and left her unsettled.

Seeing Tom will help. He might still be in the lecture theatre.

That's stalking.

No, it's not! I have to walk past it to go home.

Opening the door and looking in isn't part of your way home. What happened to getting a grip?

She conceded that point to her conscience. Her time with Tom had been wonderful, but it probably wasn't going to happen again and this jumpy-heart stuff was just fatigue.

As she gathered her jacket, bag and MP3 player out of her locker, acid burned her gut and she realised she hadn't eaten anything more than almonds and chocolate in hours. The thought of a breakfast of bacon, eggs, tomato, sausages and golden buttered toast had her salivating. She checked her watch. Twelve twenty p.m. There was only one place she knew that served breakfast until midafternoon and that was Café Luna, which was a long drive from The Harbour but only a short ferry ride away.

You need to sleep and then study.

Her stomach groaned so loudly that the nurse at a locker further down the room turned around and laughed.

'You better get something to eat fast or you'll need peppermint water for wind pain.'

Hayley joined in the laughter. 'I think you might be right.' She couldn't sleep or study on an empty stomach and if she listened to some lectures on her MP3 player during the journey there and back, that would justify the travel time. Decision made, she slammed her locker shut, shoved white earbuds into her ears and started walking.

Tom had asked Jared to drop him off at a café he'd once visited frequently but hadn't visited since the accident. He'd told Jared that he'd catch a taxi home because he didn't want him to miss out on any classes. Jared, to his credit, hadn't questioned him about why he wanted to come to this out-of-the-way place, given it was a bit of a drive, which was fortunate because Tom wasn't certain he had an answer that made much sense. All he knew was that he'd woken up that morning and had instantly thought about the little beach café. Lately, when he'd been teaching the medical students, he'd experienced odd moments of total focus—the sort of intensity he'd known when he'd been operating. It surprised him because he wasn't at all certain he wanted to teach long-term, but then again he had few other options within medicine and when he thought about working outside medicine, nothing sprang to mind.

Focus in today's lecture, however, had been seriously lacking because the idea of the café had kept interrupting him. By the time he'd answered the final question, it was like the memory of the café had taken hold of him and was demanding to be visited.

Before the accident, he'd often ridden his bike here on a Sunday morning and then he'd sit and read the papers and watch the world go by while gorging himself on the best breakfast in Sydney. Those happy memories had filled him with a zip of anticipation so by the time he'd taken his seat at his favourite outdoor table, he was almost excited. It wasn't an emotion he experienced much any more because the *one* thing that had excited him beyond anything in his life had been surgery and now that was denied him.

Thirty minutes after taking his seat, it wasn't going well. The coffee was still as aromatic and full of the caffeine kick he remembered, and the eggs on the crisply toasted English muffins were deliciously runny and the hollandaise sauce decadently creamy, but he couldn't read the paper and the sounds and smells of the busy café dominated, preventing him from getting any sense of the beach despite it only being three steps away.

The cacophony disoriented him and he hated that. He cursed himself for getting into this position. He should have asked Jared to stay. *No.* What he should have done was not given in to a stupid memory and come to the café. He knew better than giving in to memories because he couldn't relive anything any more. Nothing was ever the same now he'd lost his sight and right now was a perfect example of why he never acted on impulse. When he did, it left him stranded in unfamiliar environments and dependent on others.

'Ah, sir?' The waitress sounded uncertain.

Tom looked towards her, not because he could see her but because he knew sighted people needed him to look at them or else they thought he wasn't listening. In fact, he'd heard her footsteps well before she'd spoken, although he hadn't been certain they belonged to the waitress due to so much passing foot traffic. 'Yes?'

'Can I get you anything else? We've got some lovely cakes today.'

'I'll have another coffee. Are you busy today?'

'You arrived at the peak of the rush, but it'll be quiet again soon. I'll be right back with your espresso.'

He leaned back in the chair and breathed in, trying again to smell the sea, and this time, instead of the dominating smell of onions, bacon, coriander and chocolate, he caught a whiff of salt. He heard the excited shout of a child, but any responding voices were drowned out by an almighty crash of crockery. He sighed. Ironically, he'd never noticed any noise in the café when his entire perspective of the world had been absorbed through the visual.

His coffee arrived at the same time he heard the rumble of a ferry's engine and the cheery toot of the horn. Soon after, just as the waitress had predicted, the café quietened, which allowed the sounds of the beach to finally drift in and the salt on the air make his nostrils tingle. A second later he caught the sudden scent of summer flowers and his gut tightened.

A woman in the café or walking past on the beach was wearing the same perfume as Hayley.

Damn it. He'd managed not to think about her very often today, but it didn't take much to bring her front and centre in his mind. He'd been battling errant thoughts of Hayley for five long days, which made no sense to him at all. In the past, although he'd enjoyed his encounters with women, he'd never thought about them afterwards and he'd never had his thoughts interrupted by memories of them.

He heard a woman's voice from somewhere off to his left. 'Oh! You've dropped your teddy. Here you are.'

Tom's head swung toward the voice, which sounded identical to Hayley's.

You're totally losing it. Let's look at the facts. 1. Other women have been known to wear that perfume. 2. You're nowhere near the hospital or where she lives so that rules out Hayley. He reached out his fingers, feeling for the edge of the saucer in preparation for picking up the small coffee cup.

Noise buzzed behind him—murmured thanks, the squeak of wheels, possibly from a stroller, and then soft footsteps. Jerky almost. The exact same stop-start gait he'd heard the night he'd met Hayley on the way to the car park.

Stop it.

He ran his hand through his hair, pulling at the short strands as if that slight pain would shake the ridiculous thoughts from his head.

A cloud of coconut and floral scent floated over him and he gripped the edge of the table. He had no clue who was standing near him, and yet everything in him screamed it was Hayley. A bitter surge of vitriol at his useless eyes duelled with the surge of heat that rolled through him, taunting him with the memory of what he'd been doing the last time he'd breathed in that combination of fragrances.

'Tom? What on earth are you doing here?'

Hayley. She sounded stunned, indignant and happy all at the same time. He understood the emotions exactly. He somehow got this throat to work. 'Having breakfast for lunch.'

She laughed. 'That's why I'm here. I finished work and all I could think about was the big breakfast. May I join you?'

Say no now to avoid problems later. 'Sure.'

'Great.'

He started to move so he could stand up for her, but she said, 'There's a stroller wedged in behind you. Have you eaten?'

He welcomed her matter-of-fact tone of voice and how she'd just slipped in the information quietly without making a fuss and then continued with her conversation. 'I had the eggs Benedict.'

'Ohh, fancy. I'm going for straight grease today with an extra side of hash browns. It's crazy but sometimes I dream about these breakfasts and when I do I think it's my body telling me that I need some salt and fat.'

He remembered her delectable curves and how he'd appreciated them, unlike the feel of a woman who fought with food. He grinned. 'Sounds reasonable to me.'

She quickly gave her order to the waitress and sighed.

'Problem?'

'No, not at all.' She sounded relaxed and happy. 'It was a catching-my-breath sigh.'

He knew what she meant. 'I used to do that here.'

'Used to? Simple deduction tells me you're still doing it.'

He shook his head. 'Today's the first time I've been here in over two years.' He expected his words to be greeted with an embarrassed silence due to the indirect reference to his accident. Instead, he heard the creak of her chair as she moved in it.

'I love coming to this café and here's a perfect example why. There's an elderly couple walking hand in hand along the pier. They're deep in conversation and wearing hiking boots so I guess they're going to walk to the next cove along the cliff-top path. To your left, on the beach, there's a little boy about three and he's trying to wrestle a bright red ball from his toddler sister.'

He heard a high-pitched squeal. 'I gather the sister doesn't want to give up the ball.'

Hayley laughed and the rich, smoky sound carried both the warmth and softness of velvet. 'No, she's holding on tight and he's just sat on her. Their mother, who's on her mobile phone, hasn't paused her conversation for a second. She's just picked him up by the back of his T-shirt and he's flailing his arms and legs about.' She dropped her voice. 'Just behind you is a boy who looks about eighteen. He's got heavily tattooed arms, piercings on his face, but he's cuddling a puppy as if it's the most precious thing in the world.'

Tom instantly remembered the dog he'd adopted as a child and how devastated he'd been when it had died. His father had taken off when he'd been a baby and had never made contact again. Although his mother had loved him, she'd loved the contents of a bottle more. The dog, however, had loved him unconditionally and he could understand why the tough-looking young man was showing the puppy affection. The animal was probably the only thing in his life that gave him positive vibes. 'What sort of dog is it?'

The screeching scrape of the chair legs against concrete sounded and then he heard Hayley saying, 'Excuse me. Could we have a look at your puppy, please?'

He tensed. 'Hell, Hayley I didn't mean you to—'

But Hayley ignored him and starting talking to someone he assumed was the tattooed young man.

'Oh, he's just gorgeous,' she cooed. 'He's going to be a huge dog if he grows into those feet. This is my friend,

Tom. He's blind but he wanted to know what sort of dog it is.'

'Do you wanna hold him, mate?'

Tom suddenly felt the wriggling, warm softness of a puppy being shoved into his lap and he quickly brought his hands up to support and contain the dog. Its heart pounded hard and fast against his hand, and a wet tongue licked his thumb. He smiled as he traced the outline of its big, silky ears.

The waitress's brisk steps hurried to their table and with a clanking slam a plate hit the tabletop. 'Here's your big breakfast and no dogs are allowed in the café.'

'Technically, we're outside and this young man is on the beach so he's not in the café,' Hayley replied mildly. 'And Tom's blind so by law you have to allow his dog.'

Tom stifled a laugh at the ludicrous argument and heard the waitress's sharp intake of breath.

'That's not a seeing-eye dog.'

'Not yet.' Hayley had that tone in her voice that dared the waitress to prove her wrong. 'A great deal of training happens before a dog is old enough to wear the harness and it all starts when they're this young. It's important that they're out and about amongst people.'

Somehow Tom managed to keep a straight face and nod as well, adding gravitas to what was an outright lie. 'We have to see if we get along.'

The puppy laid its head against his forearm as he stroked the length of its back.

'Just keep it contained, okay?' The waitress walked away, her shoes slapping the ground crossly.

'Can I have me dog back now?' the young man asked.

'Sure.' Tom held the puppy out toward the voice.

'Thanks. I enjoyed the cuddle.'

'No worries. See ya.'

'Bye,' Hayley said with a smile in her voice.

Tom leaned forward, propelled toward her by a lightness of being he hadn't experienced in years—if ever. 'So tell me. What sort of a mutt were you trying to pass off as a potential seeing-eye dog?'

Her laugh matched his. 'What sort of dog did you feel?'

He thought about the picture he'd painted in his mind. 'Drop ears, wide head, long snout, strong legs, big paws, short coat and a healthy wet nose.'

'Exactly.' He heard the scratch of cutlery on china and a soft sigh of delight as she tasted her food. 'You wanted to know what sort of dog it was and now you've seen it.'

A spark of frustration flared. 'I have no clue of its colour.'

'A gorgeous golden blond.'

Her perfume eddied around him and he realised she'd leaned forward. He fought against the distraction and thought about the dog and its short coat and immediately ruled out a golden retriever. 'You've got to be kidding me. That dog was actually a golden Labrador?'

'I know you want to cast me as a con artist and, granted, I was pushing the envelope, but technically that dog could have been a trainee guide dog. Besides, you looked happy and we weren't upsetting any customers. I would have said the same thing if it had been a Jack Russell.'

He fought the traitorous cosy feeling of being cared for by using the stark reality of abandonment as the weapon. Experience had taught him not to let himself be tricked by caring because it always let him down. A long sigh shuddered out of him. 'Hayley.'

She responded with an exaggerated sigh. 'Tom.'

It made him want to smile, but it was time to be frank. Time to lay his cards on the table and kill any illusions she might have about the two of them. 'About the other day. You do know it wasn't the start of anything between us. I've never done relationships and I don't intend to start now. It was what it was. Great sex.' He heard her put her cutlery down and he braced himself for her reply. He'd had this conversation before.

'I'm glad we agree. It *was* great sex. Nothing more and nothing less so now you can stop worrying that I've booked the church and put a deposit on a dress.'

He wished he could see her face—see if her expression matched her voice, which sounded very normal and without the strain of a lie. But he wasn't totally convinced. Before he'd lost his sight he'd never met a woman who hadn't held a hint of hope in her eyes that a relationship would grow from a casual fling.

Her hand settled over his, her fingers stroking the back of his hand. 'I can see you don't believe me, but you should. I like you, Tom, but I've got exams looming and my whole life at the moment is work and study. I hardly have any time to sleep, my parents have taken to visiting me in the cafeteria at The Harbour because I can never manage to get home to see them, so if I can't even manage that, I know I don't have the time or the energy to give to a relationship. But…'

The 'but' worried him. However, her touch had his pulse racing and it took every bit of willpower he had not to link his fingers with hers. 'But what?'

She doodled lazy circles around each knuckle. 'You remember what it was like just before you qualified?'

Through the growing fog of desire that was building inside him, he located a memory. 'Sheer hell.'

'Exactly. Stress city, and it's well documented that sex releases tension and I have a very stressful time coming up.'

Was he hearing right? He didn't dare to believe it so

he asked, 'Are you saying you want to have sex without the relationship part?'

Her other hand linked fingers with his. 'Ever heard of friends with benefits?'

He had. 'I didn't think it really existed.'

She laughed. 'Oh, it does. It works well for busy people. Unlike a relationship, we're not at each other's beck and call, but when it suits us both we get together. A sort of win-win situation.'

She's right about the final year of surgery. There's no time for anything other than work.

There'll be a catch. Women don't suggest this sort of thing. Guys do.

But the memory of being buried deep in Hayley was so strong and the thought of being there again was so tempting that it stampeded over the faint echoes of his concerns.

'When do we start?'

CHAPTER EIGHT

'I SHOULD go.' Hayley sat forward, having spent the last twenty minutes leaning back on Tom's chest as he sat propped up against a tree.

Two weeks had passed since she'd run into Tom at Café Luna. Seeing him sitting alone in the café had brought up a mix of contrary emotions, starting with shocked surprise, moving into relief and then finishing up with something that made her feel unexpectedly bereft at the thought of not seeing him again. That had propelled her to suggest being 'friends with benefits'. It was the perfect solution. Obvious even.

She knew what she was getting into and it wasn't like she'd never done it before. It suited her and if the past fortnight was anything to go by, it was the best decision she'd made in a long time. Not that they'd seen a lot of each other, but when they could coordinate their schedules, the sex had been as wondrous as their first time. Still, as amazing as the sex always was, it was times like the hour they'd just spent having a picnic in the park close to her cottage that she was really starting to treasure. They could talk for hours about all sorts of things and equally she could sit in companionable silence with him and not feel the need to talk. She hadn't experienced anything close to that sort of ease with someone since Amy.

Tom's arm, which had been resting casually across her chest, tightened against her and he nuzzled her neck. 'Come back to my place.'

She turned and pressed her lips to his, loving that she could do that whenever they were alone. 'Later. First I have to do another three hours of study and then you're my treat for working hard. Will you be home about seven?'

'Tonight, yes.' He stroked her hair. 'It seems I'm surrounded by people who are studying.'

'How's Jared going?' She'd enjoyed helping the young man with the chemistry and had appreciated his rough but honest manner.

'He's working hard.'

It was the perfect segue to ask the question she'd long pondered. 'How did Jared go from being your patient to your friend?'

The edges of Tom's mouth tightened a fraction. 'I don't really know, but it was probably because he wouldn't go away and now I'm stuck with him.'

But although he might think he sounded resigned and put upon, she saw his affection for the young man shining clearly on his face. 'What's the real story?'

The doctor moved to front and centre. 'I clipped an aneurysm in his brain two months before I left for Perth. He came through Outpatients as a public patient and he was a bright kid, but, like a lot of kids from the western suburbs, life wasn't easy and he had a massive chip on his shoulder. I don't think I got more than grunts out of him before the operation.'

She smiled. 'And let me guess, you chatted to him just like you talked to Gretel.'

Two deep lines carved into a V at the bridge of his nose. 'I talked to him like I talk to all my patients.'

She shrugged. 'Maybe you think you did, but I find

some patients are easier to deal with than others. You might not realise it but you have a knack with young people.'

'No, I don't.'

'Yeah, you do. Look at the medical students. It's standing room only at your guest lecture spots.'

'Only because they'll be failed if they don't turn up.'

She dug him in the ribs with her elbow—half joking and half serious. 'That's not the only reason and you know it. You're a good lecturer because you speak to them, not at them.'

A muscle twitched in his jaw. 'I'd rather be operating.'

She flinched, absorbing the hit of his pain, but then she took the reality road—a path she'd always taken with him because she knew the 'if only' road was a dead end filled with unrelenting despair. 'I know you'd rather be operating, but you can't so why not embrace this avenue of medicine? You enjoy young people's company, you must or you wouldn't have Jared over at your place so often.'

His shoulders rose and fell. 'I think I must have seen something in Jared that reminded me of myself at a similar age. That and the fact he lives five streets away from where I grew up.'

She recalled the comment he'd made about her Northern Beaches upbringing. 'And that wasn't the Northern Beaches?'

His laugh was harsh and abrupt. 'As far from there as you can possibly get.'

She wanted to know. 'Where?'

'Derrybrook Estate.'

She'd heard of it, but had never been there. 'What's it like?'

'It's got the highest unemployment rate in the city, is a

hub for crime and drugs, and most kids drop out of school by sixteen.'

She thought about his polished veneer and how whenever he was angry or stressed it cracked, exposing the rough edges he'd obviously worked hard at smoothing over. Now it all made sense. She found herself imagining a struggling family with a bright son. 'Studies have shown that no matter the economic circumstances, if a family values education that's the one thing that makes the difference.'

He flinched and his high cheekbones sharpened. 'I wouldn't know about that. The fact I stayed at school had absolutely *nothing* to do with my family.'

His words stung like a slap. 'Oh. I just assumed that—'

'Yeah, well, don't.' He flattened his spine against the tree as if he wanted to move away from her.

'I'm sorry. Obviously, though, you not only finished school, you went on to have a brilliant career.'

'Had.'

'Do.' She didn't realise she could sound so much like a school teacher. 'The fact it's different doesn't make it any less.'

'If you say so.'

She knew he didn't believe her and she ached for him because for some reason he didn't seem to recognise that he was a great teacher. 'Can you just answer my original question, please?'

The stubble on his now drawn-in cheeks made him look thunderous and she wondered if he was going to say anything more. She'd just about given up when he spoke.

'You're not going to stop asking, are you?'

'No.'

He sighed. 'At fourteen, I hated school. I was bored by everything and I was heading straight toward the juvenile justice system. Ironically, the fact I was acting out saved me.'

She wanted to know everything but all parts of her screamed at her to go slowly. If she rushed him for information, he'd clam up. As hard as it was to stay silent, she managed it, but only just.

His haggard expression softened. 'One night the football coach caught me on the roof of the school with cans of spray paint in my hand. I was seconds away from graffitiing the windows. It wasn't the first time I'd been in trouble, but instead of calling the police, he held it over me and made me go to training. I hated him for it, but at the same time part of me wanted to go. I hated being there but I missed it when I wasn't, and it confused the hell out of me. The fact Mick put up with my smart mouth and gave me more than one chance was a miracle and once I started to achieve in footy, I started to settle at school and attended regularly.'

'But I don't understand. With your brain, why were you bored by school?' The question slipped out before she could stop it.

He snorted. 'You went to an all-girls private school, didn't you?'

His accusatory tone bit into her. 'I did but—'

He held up his hand. 'Don't give me "buts". You had teachers who cared, parents who valued education and facilities that weren't broken or falling down around your ears.'

She sat up straight, propelled by a mixture of guilt and anger. He made her childhood sound idyllic and what it had been was so far from that it didn't bear thinking about. 'By the sounds of things, *you* had a teacher who cared.'

'Yeah. I had a couple.' He sighed. 'Mick's wife, Carol, was a maths and science teacher. Looking back, I now see what they really did for me. What I thought was a casual invitation of "come home for dinner" after footy training was really "we'll give you a healthy meal, a quiet place to study and any help you need". *They're* the reason I passed year twelve and got into medicine. That, and a burning desire to prove the bastards wrong.'

His pain swamped her and she instinctively pressed her hand to his heart. He'd not once mentioned his parents. 'Which bastards?'

The set of his shoulders and the grimness around his mouth reminded her of the first time she'd met him when he'd been practising navigating around the hospital. 'Everyone who ever told me I wouldn't amount to anything because my mother was drunk more than she was sober. Her drinking started when my father took off, leaving her a single mother at seventeen and gradually got worse after every other man she'd tried to love did the same thing. Everyone who's still telling kids from the estate the same thing.'

'I bet Mick and Carol were really proud of you.'

He swallowed and seemed to force the words up and out from a very deep place. 'Mick never saw me graduate. He died when I was in fifth year, taken out hard and fast by a glioblastoma, the most aggressive type of brain tumour a person can have.'

'Oh, I'm so sorry.' But she suddenly understood. 'And that's why you drove yourself to be a neurosurgeon.'

He nodded as if he was lost in the clutch of memories and then his lips formed a quiet smile. 'For Mick first and then for the Ferrari.'

She smiled and slid her hand into his. 'Proving the bastards wrong?'

He gripped it hard. 'Hell, yeah.'

Her own heart swelled as she glimpsed the man's giving heart that he seemed to want to hide more often than not. 'So now you're paying it forward and giving Jared the same sort of support that Mick and Carol gave you?'

He shook his head. 'Carol was born to help, but I'm no saint, Hayley. I didn't seek Jared out or offer to mentor him, like Mick did for me. Jared tracked me down in Perth and then refused to go away.'

'But now you're helping him. He probably tracked you down because of how you related to him when he was sick.'

The admiration in Hayley's voice couldn't be mistaken for anything else, but Tom didn't want to hear it. Their conversation had taken him far too close to the memories of his mother. Hell, he hated thinking about her because it took him back to a place he'd fought so hard to escape. Hayley had no clue about the eroding nature of abject poverty. How it slowly ate away at self-esteem and corroded hope, making the seduction of alcohol and drugs so tantalising as a temporary escape.

Only it wasn't an escape at all. It was an extension of the poverty trap, which then gripped people like his mother permanently until death claimed them. Her death had been her release and he ached that she'd wanted death more than she'd ever wanted him.

He shivered as he pushed the memories away and then realised the wind had changed. He reached out his hand for his cane. 'Feel the cold in that wind? What does the sky look like?'

'Gunmetal.' She shivered. 'Oh, it's really spooky.'

He heard her tossing things into the picnic hamper as the sun vanished. The temperature plummeted and the south-buster wind picked up speed. Dust made his eyes water and he could imagine the leaves and any debris being tossed every which way by the ferocious wind that howled around them.

He stood up and wished he knew the area better. 'We need to find shelter.'

'My place is less than two blocks away.'

He shook his head. 'I know storms like this and we don't have that much time.'

As if on cue, huge drops of rain started falling, but the violence of the wind blew them horizontally, stinging his face.

'Ouch.' Hayley caught his hand. 'Since when does rain hurt?'

'When it's sleet. I was here in 1999 for Sydney's most expensive hailstorm ever and this feels like the start of that.' He yelled to be heard over the wind. 'Get us to the nearest shelter. Now.'

Thunder cracked around them and Hayley squealed. 'Sorry.' She jammed his hand on her shoulder. 'There's a bandstand a hundred metres away.'

As they started walking, the sleet became hail—stones of ice that dive-bombed them with sharp edges, and stung, bruised and grazed any uncovered skin. It was the most painful hundred metres he'd ever walked and he hated that his blindness meant Hayley had to endure it too instead of being able to run to safety.

'Three steps,' Hayley yelled over the noise of the hail on the bandstand's tin roof.

He navigated the steps and he knew he must be inside the bandstand, but they were still being pummelled by hail. Bandstands generally had only hip-height walls, which gave scant protection when the wind was driving the hail in at a thirty-degree angle. 'We need to get down and huddle.'

'We can sit on the ground wedged in against the seat.

That puts us lower than the height of the wall.' She moved his hand and he felt wooden slats before he lowered himself down and sat cross-legged on the wet and icy concrete.

Another crack of thunder seemed almost overhead and Hayley's arms wrapped around his head so tightly he risked neck damage. He reached out and wet strands of her hair plastered themselves against his palm. 'I gather you don't like thunder.'

She shivered against him. 'I think I must have been a dog in a previous life.'

'Get the picnic rug out and we'll use it as extra protection.'

'Okay.' She sounded uncertain but she pulled away from him.

He heard her cold fingers fumbling to untie the toggles, followed by the emphatic use of a swear word he'd never heard her say. In fact, he'd never heard her swear, not even in the OR when she'd been operating on Gretel. She really was scared. The next minute she scrambled into his lap and her whole body trembled against his as she wrapped the rug around their shoulders. 'I hate this.'

'I'm getting that impression, but usually storms like this are over quickly.' He stroked her wet back as an unfamiliar surge of protectiveness filled him and then he pulled the rug over their heads to protect their faces.

Her fingernails instantly dug into his scalp as sharp and as tenacious as a cat's claws. 'Hell, Hayley, what are you doing?'

But she didn't speak. Instead, her chest heaved hard and fast against his and the next moment she'd torn back the rug and was panting hard.

He reached out his hand, trying to feel the rug. 'We need the protection.'

'You have it.' She threw the rug over his head and he immediately blew it away from his mouth. The instinctive action made him think. 'Are you claustrophobic as well as scared of the dark?'

There was a moment's silence before she said, 'It's easing. The hail's turned into rain.' She grabbed his hand. 'Let's go to my place. Please.'

The pleading in her voice both surprised him and propelled him to his feet. 'Lead the way.'

As they reached the bottom of the bandstand's steps, Hayley said, 'I can't believe some hailstones are the size of cricket balls.'

'I'll trudge, then.'

After navigating flooded gutters and hail-covered footpaths for five minutes, Hayley said, 'We turn left and then we're home. It's a tiny cottage and nothing like your penthouse.'

The rain was now trickling down Tom's collar and the cold seeped into his bones. So much for mild Sydney winters. Still, perhaps the storm wasn't all bad. He now had the perfect excuse to entice Hayley into bed—he needed to keep warm while his clothes dried in front of her heater. Then he'd go home and leave her to her study.

With a loud gasp Hayley suddenly stopped and he crashed into her as water flowed over his feet. 'Is your house flooded?'

'I don't think so. The water hasn't quite reached the front door.'

'You might want to make a bit of a levee between the front door and the road, then.' He kept his hand on her shoulder, following her, all the while trying to tamp down his rising frustration that he had no idea what she was seeing and that the only help he could give was advice.

He heard her slide a key into a lock and then the grating squeak of a door swinging open.

'Oh, God.' She pulled away from him and the sound of her running feet against bare boards echoed around him, leaving him with the impression he was standing in a long corridor. Her wail of despair carried back to him.

'Hayley?' Using his cane, he tapped his way along the corridor. 'What's happened?'

'My roof's collapsed, my windows are almost all broken and I have a house full of hail.' She sounded utterly defeated.

Tom instantly recalled the billion-dollar damage that the huge storm of 1999 had inflicted on the city. He pulled out his phone. 'Show me where I can sit down and I'll call the State Emergency Services to come and tarpaulin your roof, and then I'll wait in the phone queue of your insurance company. They're going to be inundated so it might take a while and you can sweep up the hail.'

'I don't even know where to start.' Her voice rose with every word. 'There's more plaster on the floor than on the ceiling and I can see sky!'

Seeing sky wasn't good. He ran his hand through his hair. 'You can't stay here, then, even with a tarpaulin.'

He heard a chair being pulled out and a thud. 'What a mess. I really don't need this with my exams looming. My parents live too far out for me to get to the hospital when I'm on call so I guess I'm going to have to find a motel.'

Tom didn't like her chances. 'You'll be lucky to find a place if every house is as badly affected as yours.'

'Are you trying to cheer me up?'

He could imagine the mess she was sitting amidst and his heart went out to her. Before he'd thought it through he heard himself saying, 'Go pack up your textbooks and computer, throw some clothes in a bag and come back to my place.'

What the hell have you just done? You live alone. You've always lived alone. More than ever you need to live alone.

I can't just leave her here and it will only be a few days. I can handle a few days.

Her hand touched his cheek and then her lips pressed hard against his mouth. 'Thank you. I'm so glad you're here bossing me around because I'm not sure I would have known where to start.'

'Bossing people around is what I do best.' He dug deep and managed to muster up a smile to cover how useless he felt and how he hated it that he couldn't do more. Once he would have been on the roof, lashing down the tarpaulins, or wielding a broom and sweeping out the mud and muck left by flood waters or removing sodden plaster. Now all he could offer in the way of help was phone calls and letting her stay for a bit. It was a poor man's offer and it didn't feel like he was contributing at all.

Finn Kennedy gripped the silver arm of the pool ladder with his left hand as every muscle in his body frantically tried to absorb the lactic acid his obsessively long swim had just generated. He'd started swimming soon after the hail storm, ploughing up and down the Olympic pool, willing his neck pain away. Or at least giving the muscles in his neck some rest by supporting them in warm water. He'd rather swim for an hour than wear the damn cervical collar Rupert Davidson forced on him. It was bad enough that the staff at The Harbour were whispering about him and giving him furtive glances. He sure as hell wasn't giving them an obvious target like a soft collar so they felt they could ask him questions.

Pressing his foot into the foothold, he swung up and stepped onto the pool deck, the air feeling chilly after the heat of the water. He scooped up his towel and hurried to the locker room. He reached the door just ahead of Sam Bailey, The Harbour's cardiac surgeon, who raised his hand with a smile. Avoiding eye contact, Finn gave a brisk nod of acknowledgment before heading straight to the showers. He cranked up the hot tap until the temperature was just shy of burning and let the heat sink into his skin and the constantly stressed muscles below. After doing his neck exercises under the heat of the shower, the skill lay in getting dry and dressed fast so his clothes could trap the heat for as long as possible. It was almost as good as the anti-inflammatories and he used it once a day to stretch out *one* time period between the pills.

With his towel looped low on his hips, he quickly grabbed hold of the combination lock, spun the black dial three times and then pulled down hard to open the lock so he could retrieve his clothes. The silver U stayed locked. 'Blast.' His fingers felt thick and uncoordinated. He tried again, but still the lock stayed firm. He slammed his hand hard against the unyielding door and the crash resonated in the cavernous room.

'These locks can be bastards,' Sam said quietly, having appeared at the locker next to his. He spun his own lock slowly and methodically. 'If you don't hit the exact spot, they won't open.'

'You don't say,' Finn ground out as he tried again, feeling the sideways glance of his colleague along with the fast-fading power of the heat from the shower. Beads of sweat formed on his forehead and one trickled down into his eye. Hell, he was a surgeon. He could sew the finest and smallest stitches so that his patient was left virtually scar-free. He sure as hell could open a bloody lock.

A registrar rescued you when you couldn't tie off that bleeder.

That was once. It hasn't happened again.

It's happening now.

His fingers on his right hand were doing exactly what they'd done during that operation and he couldn't control their gross movements let alone make them execute a fine task. He brought his left hand up to the lock, and in what seemed like slow motion he finally got it to open.

Sam slammed his locker shut. 'Will I see you in the gym?'

Finn shook his head. 'I'm done.'

'Catch you later, then.'

Finn didn't reply. With a pounding heart he pulled his clothes on, wrapped a scarf around his neck and with legs that felt weak he sank onto the wooden bench between the lockers, dropping his head in his hands.

You can't even open a blasted lock.

He rubbed his arm and swore at the offending fingers. He couldn't deny it was happening more often—this loss of sensation that had him dropping things. Hell, he'd already had some time off and rested exactly as Rupert had suggested. He hated following instructions, but he'd done everything the neurosurgeon had suggested. On his return to work he'd cut back his surgery hours so he wasn't standing for long periods. He'd taken up swimming, he'd even tried Pilates, which galled him, and none of it was working. He was still swallowing analgesia tablets like they were lollies and he refused to think about his Scotch intake.

He ran his left hand over the back of his neck, locating the offending area between cervical vertebrae five and six. Wasn't it enough that the bomb had killed Isaac, stealing his only brother from him? Apparently not. Its remnants now lingered with him way beyond the pain of grief. The blast that had knocked him sideways, rendering him unconscious, had jarred his neck so badly that the soft nucleus of the cushioning disc now bulged outwards, putting pressure on the spinal cord. That something so small could cause so much chaos was beyond ironic. It was sadistic and it threatened to steal from him the one thing that kept him getting up in the mornings. His reason for living. The one true thing that defined him.

Surgery.

So far he'd been lucky. So far he'd been able to survive without mishap the few times his weak arm and numb fingers had caused him to stumble in surgery. So far his patients hadn't suffered at his unreliable hand and they wouldn't because he now made sure he only operated with a registrar present.

His gut sent up a fire river of acid and his chest constricted as the horrifying thought he'd long tried to keep at bay voiced itself in his head.

How long can you really keep operating?

CHAPTER NINE

HAYLEY was exhausted, but at least she was now warm. It always amazed her how therapeutic a hot shower could be. She'd finally got back to Tom's place at eight p.m., after the SES guys had boarded up her windows and lashed a tarpaulin over her roof. She still couldn't believe that ten minutes of freaky weather could wreak so much havoc. She smiled and hugged herself whenever she thought of how Tom had quietly and methodically organised things, including helping her neighbour, a single mother with a young baby. Thea had rushed in crying and he'd calmed her down, asked Hayley to make tea for everyone and had then made phone calls for her as well.

Hayley knew that if she'd been on her own she would have made herself cope with everything, but having Tom deal with the SES and the insurance company while she busied herself with the practical clean-up had made it all much more bearable. They'd made a great team, but whenever she'd tried to tell him that and thank him, his mouth had flattened into a grimace and he'd brushed her appreciation aside. Oddly, he'd accepted Thea's thanks with grace, which Hayley didn't understand at all, and it had left her feeling disgruntled.

Hunger had her quickly brushing her hair and padding out to the main living area, which was cloaked in darkness except for the glow of Tom's computer screen. She automatically reached for the light switches and flicked them all on.

Tom immediately turned toward her and smiled. 'My light bill has plummeted since I went blind.'

She jumped. 'I'll pay the electricity bill while I'm here.'

He frowned. 'I was making a joke, Hayley.'

She forced out a laugh because as far as she was concerned the dark was *nothing* to joke about. She crossed the room and, with her heart racing, quickly closed the curtains. Despite the pretty twinkling lights, there was too much dark around them and it made her feel anxious. Shutting out the night was an evening ritual for her no matter where she was so she could bathe in the glow of artificial light and pretend it wasn't dark at all.

Her stomach rumbled and she said brightly, 'Do you actually cook with that flash stainless-steel gas stove or is it just for decoration?'

'Even with the lights on, can't you enjoy the night view of the city lights?'

The quietly asked question was tinged with surprise and it made her shiver. 'Of course I can, but it's cold tonight so I'm keeping the heat in.' She sucked in a breath and rushed on. 'Theo, at work, he's been hammering us with sustainable living information and closing curtains at night cuts greenhouse gas emissions and saves you money. So, what are we doing about dinner? I'm starving.'

He closed his laptop. 'I have three recipes I can manage in emergencies, but Gladys keeps my freezer filled with her home-cooked specialities, which has made me a brilliant defroster and re-heater. I'm also excellent at ordering take-out and dining at Wayan's.' He rose to his feet and walked into the kitchen, his gait the most relaxed she'd ever seen it. 'Prepare yourself for a treat. Tonight we're having Gladys's tasty beef and ginger.'

She followed him. 'Do you want me to cook the rice? Boiling water is my speciality.'

'You're on.' He felt for a particular drawer handle, pulled it open, picked up a saucepan and handed it to her with a cheeky and generous smile.

Dimples twirled through his ebony stubble and part of her melted as it did every time he smiled. But this smile was extra-special because it wasn't one she saw very often. It didn't carry the vestiges of pain or grief, neither did it hold the rigid determination of striving to be independent at all costs. No, this smile was pure Tom and it spun around her heart like gossamer thread.

Tom woke with a jolt of surprise, wondering what on earth was pinning his legs to the bed. He breathed in the scent of summer flowers and instantly remembered. Hailstorm, damaged house, and Hayley was in his bed. He stretched out his arm and touched an empty mattress. He kept going until his hand brushed her shoulder and he realised she was lying diagonally across the bed. Was this why she'd never stayed the night, because she was either a bed-hog or had restless-leg syndrome?

You never invited her to stay.

True.

But then it hit him that up until this evening they'd mostly had sex during the day because she'd been doing more than her fair share of night shifts. The one time they'd had sex at night she'd seemed eager to return home and he'd had no quarrel with that. Sex and friendship was one thing. Her toothbrush in his bathroom was another thing entirely.

She's living here.

No, she's staying here temporarily.

He disentangled himself from her legs and rolled over with the intention of falling straight back to sleep but something made him stare towards the door. It was the middle of the night, but he could see a shadow. He blinked and looked again. It was still there, so he rubbed his eyes. The shadow didn't shift, which meant the room wasn't totally dark like it should be in middle of the night. Had he slept so soundly that it was morning?

He reached for his talking clock but then changed his mind because he didn't want to wake up Hayley. He patted the bedside table, feeling for his watch, and his hand collided with the recently replaced lamp. Why the hell had he let Gladys talk him into that? 'Ouch.' His fingers instantly pulled away. The lamp was unexpectedly hot.

Hayley's legs twitched, hitting his, and he sat up, leaning back against the headboard. *Just think this through.*

Being confused about his surroundings happened out in the world, but it never happened in his apartment. This was his sanctuary. He knew where everything was and he knew all the familiar shadows and the times of day they appeared. He also knew all the noises, from the gurgling water in the pipes to the four a.m. clunk of the freezer. The shadow by the doorway hadn't been there when he'd fallen asleep and he knew the lamp hadn't been on because when they'd come to bed Hayley had suggested switching it on and he'd thought it irrelevant and had distracted her by trailing kisses down her neck and beyond. He grinned at how easy she was to distract and at the same time loving how responsive she was whenever he touched her.

The lamp is hot.

Which meant it was turned on. He swung his legs out of bed, pulled on some boxers and walked to the doorway. He ran his hand along the architrave and found the light switch. Touching it lightly so as not to move it, he worked out the switch was pointing down. He automatically scratched his head. He'd assumed that her fear of the dark only worried her when she was awake and in an unfamiliar environment. His apartment was hardly unfamiliar so why was she sleeping in a fully lit room? No wonder Hayley was restless.

He turned the lights out, made his way back to the bedside table and switched off the lamp. Then he got back into bed and Hayley rolled into him with a groan and her legs thrashing wildly. The groan wasn't ecstatic—it was guttural and reminded him of pain. Whatever the dream she was having, it wasn't happy. He threw his leg over both of hers with the intention of stilling them, and as he gathered her to him, he felt her body slick with sweat.

He found her head and tried to stroke her temple, but she was writhing about too much and he caught a sharp elbow to the jaw. He swore.

'Amy!' Hayley screamed, and stiffened in his arms, her chest heaving as if she'd run a marathon.

He gave her a small shake. 'Hayley, it's okay. Wake up, it's just a dream.'

He heard her gasp, felt her body-length shudder and smelled her fear. Then she was out of bed, her bare feet slapping the floor, and the next thing he heard was the click of the light switch.

He instantly remembered her stop-start feet the night he'd met her, her reaction when the rug had gone over her head, and how she'd been turning lights on all night. And now this. Her reaction went beyond fear and edged on being petrified.

'Hayley, what's going on?'

She couldn't get her breath and she wanted to sink to

the floor, cuddle her knees and rock back and forth. Her recurring nightmare was getting out of control.

You know it's been out of control for years. But admitting that out loud was too scary. 'Nothing's wrong. Just a bad dream after a big day.'

His head turned slightly to her voice and his sightless eyes stared straight at her. 'It's a hell of a lot more than that. It's connected with your fear of the dark, isn't it?'

Her chest tightened. She'd hidden this from so many people over so many years because she never let anyone get close, and yet it was a blind man who'd just worked it out. She blew out a breath, replaying his words in her head, and she realised his matter-of-fact tone held no condemnation. The part of her that always tried to hide her fear let out a tired sigh.

Tell him.

No. Reliving that night over and over in a dream was one thing. Talking about it would do her in.

It might help.

It won't.

'Remember our pact of not having to answer questions? Well, I'm invoking it.' She got back into bed and snuggled down. 'Let's go back to sleep.'

His arms gathered her close and she let herself be cocooned in his mantle of safety. Under the soothing yellow beam of the central light her eyelids fluttered downwards.

'Most of us grow out of this particular childhood fear. What happened to you that prevented it?'

Her eyes shot open. Why did he have to be so damn intuitive?

Because he isn't distracted by images.

'Nothing happened. I'm just an exception to the rule.'

He huffed out a breath. 'Sleeping with a nightlight is one thing. Sleeping under the glare of three sixty-watt bulbs is another thing entirely. I live in semi-darkness, Hayley, it's not that scary.'

She instinctively shuddered at the thought and then regretted it.

His lips grazed her shoulder. 'Who's Amy?'

No way. No. She threw back the covers as panic consumed her. 'Go back to sleep, Tom.'

She grabbed her pyjamas and rushed towards the kitchen, flinging on lights wherever she saw a switch until the entire apartment was lit up like a Christmas tree. With trembling hands she filled the kettle and set it to boil and then she frantically opened cupboards, searching for some sort of soothing tea.

'What are you looking for?' Tom stood in a pair of boxers and a T-shirt that fitted his toned chest like a glove and made him look like an underwear model.

But it did nothing to dent her panic. 'Chamomile tea, peppermint tea, any bloody tea!'

One corner of his mouth tweaked up. 'I don't have any.'

Ridiculous tears pricked the back of her eyes. 'That's not helpful at all.'

He put out his arm and caught hers, pulling her into him. 'How about hot milk and brandy? The nurses swear by it for calming down crazy old ladies who try to climb over the cot sides.'

Her worst fear made her sharp. 'I'm not crazy.'

His hand stroked her hair. 'Not usually, but you are tonight and I'd hazard a guess you've been like this many times before. Isn't it wearing you out?'

Yes. The sympathy in his voice unlocked something inside her and tears started to fall. 'I'm so tired, Tom. I'm so very, very tired.'

He held her, his arms circled tightly around her and he pressed kisses in her hair. She could have stayed there for ever with his strength flowing through her. She felt protected, cared for and safe in a way she hadn't felt in years. Eventually he dropped his arms and said, 'You go sit on the couch and I'll make you that milk.'

She almost said, 'I'll do it', but the determination on his face stopped her. Instead, she did as she was told and cuddled up on the couch with a light polar fleece blanket draped around her shoulders, and she came to a decision.

Tom picked up the mug of hot milk. Heating it was the easy part. Getting the damn thing to Hayley without spilling it was another thing entirely, but if he could do it anywhere it was here. Once he was out of the kitchen it was twelve steps to the couch. He started walking, concentrating on making each step smooth. 'Where are you?'

'On the right-hand side of the couch.'

He turned and counted five more steps. At least her voice sounded stronger than it had a few minutes ago and no milk had scalded his hand. Miracles could happen. He held out the mug. 'Here.'

'Thanks.' She accepted it, her fingers brushing his, and a moment later she started coughing. 'How much brandy's in this?'

Obviously too much. He hated that he had no clue how much he'd put in, and that what was supposed to be a helpful act had her coughing like an asthmatic. He sat down next to her. 'Tell me about Amy.'

She gave a long sigh. 'Amy's my…' She gulped and then her words rushed out. 'Amy was my twin sister. She died suddenly when we were eleven.'

A shock of guilt flared through him, making him regret his previous accusations that, unlike him, she'd had a perfect childhood. The guilt tumbled over empathy. Although he didn't have siblings, he'd experienced enough loss to have a form of understanding. 'I'm sorry.'

'Yeah.' She sounded sad and resigned. 'It was a long time ago. Too long ago.'

But time didn't mean squat with grief. 'Doesn't make it any easier.'

'No. I still miss her. I know that can't be right but I do.'

She paused and he wished he could see her face, but he couldn't make out anything but shadows. He heard her shudder out a breath.

'For eleven years my life was happy and relatively care-free. Amy was my best friend, my conscience and my other half. Sometimes we didn't even have to talk to find out what the other was thinking, we just knew. Once when Dad took Amy to buy me a birthday present she came home having chosen the exact same gift I had bought for her.'

He wondered what it was like to be that connected to another human being. He'd never got close. Never allowed himself to get that close.

Until now.

He shook his head against the words. 'Were you identical?'

'Yes.'

He let her silence ride, knowing she had to tell her story in her own time.

'I'm the eldest by twenty minutes and I took my job as the "big sister" very seriously.'

He smiled. 'I can picture you doing that.'

'Is that code for saying I'm bossy?'

He reached out, patting the couch until he felt her leg, which he gave a gentle squeeze. 'You know what you want and there's no crime in that.'

'I guess I've been trying to live my life for Amy too.' Her voice sounded small and she lifted his hand, folding it in hers and gripping it hard. 'One night, Amy crawled into bed with me, saying she felt weird. We'd been to a party and had eaten way too much junk food and we didn't want to confess that to Mum because she was huge on eating healthy, so I cuddled her and we both fell asleep. I woke up and my clock said 3:03. Amy was still in bed with me, only…'

Her fingers crushed his but he didn't move. He now understood exactly why she feared the dark so much and he wished he could turn back time and change what had happened to her. Change the fact she'd woken up with her sister dead in her arms. But, hell, he couldn't change a thing. He kissed her hand.

'She'd died of bacterial meningitis and I didn't even get sick.' Her voice rose on a wail and he waited, giving her a chance to compose herself.

'I was a kid and I didn't understand any of it.' Her voice sounded stronger. 'I thought it should have been me who died and for a long time I refused to accept she was dead. My parents were inconsolable and I spent a lot of years being the perfect child so as not to give them any more stress and maybe to honour Amy. I felt so guilty that she'd died and I lived. I went to school, I worked hard and achieved, but I was living in a fog. I didn't do the normal teenage stuff like parties and boyfriends, and I couldn't sleep at night. I took to napping in the day, which worked at university between lectures, and once I'd qualified, I always offered to do night shift. Over the years I've become the power-nap queen.' Her laugh was hollow. 'I worked out that if I sleep in the light the nightmares are less. As you've just found out, sleeping in the dark is an invitation for fear to invade.'

'You're chronically exhausted.' He ran his fingers over the back of her hand. She was an intelligent woman and a brilliant doctor, but she couldn't see that she also had posttraumatic stress disorder. 'You sleeping with the lights on isn't going to bother me, but you know it isn't helping you.'

The couch vibrated as she dropped his hand and shifted. 'I think I know what works best for me.'

Her defensive tone told him to back off, but he wasn't having a bar of it. 'Hayley, not very long ago you told me that you're exhausted. If you don't deal with this you're going to fall apart in a monumental breakdown and climbing back from that will be beyond hard.'

'Suddenly you're a psychiatrist?'

Her sarcasm whipped him but he let it wash over him. 'Hell, no. I treated brains with surgery, but even if I could still operate, I wouldn't be able to fix this.' He closed his eyes for a moment, seeking the strength to share something he'd never told anyone.

You never share anything with anyone.

But he knew he had to expose his own weakness to help her. 'After the accident I thought death was preferable to being blind. I couldn't see a damn thing, but when I shut my eyes I relived the accident in all its Technicolor glory. The shock of the car hitting me, the cool zip of the air as I flew through it still on my bike, and the terrifying crunching sound as my head slammed into the pavement. All of it was pushing me deep into a very black pit. Reluctantly, I agreed to hypnotherapy.'

'I can't imagine you doing that.'

He understood her surprise. 'Neither could I, but it was better than talking about my damn feelings to someone who had no bloody clue and could only look at me and think, thank God, that's not me.'

It was suddenly really important to him that she seek professional help. He wanted her to be well and get the most out of her life. He moved closer to her, smelling the citrus of her hair and using it to find her face. He traced her cheek and with his finger. 'Promise me you'll try it.'

He felt her hesitation, smelt her scepticism, apprehension and doubt, and just when he thought she'd refuse, she leaned her forehead against his and whispered, 'Thank you.'

He immediately shrugged off her heartfelt words. 'There's nothing to thank me for. I'm just doing what any friend would do.'

She sighed as if she didn't quite believe him. 'Well, thanks for caring.'

He opened his mouth to say 'You're welcome' but the words stalled in his throat as his heart suddenly ached without reason. Something in her voice had skated too close to it for comfort. *Caring?* He tried to shrug it off, tried to rationalise his wanting to help her as a normal reaction to a patient or friend. It wouldn't stick. Hayley wasn't a patient and he'd never had a friend like her.

She's special.

A flutter of panic skittered through his veins.

Hayley's fingers caressed the keys of Tom's piano, revelling in the rich sounds, and she lost herself in one of Chopin's nocturnes. As soon as her house was habitable again, she was going to buy a piano. She'd moved so much in the last ten years that she didn't own one, but this last ten days she'd found the music was helping her.

She felt Tom's hand settle on her shoulder and she leaned back into him, loving his strength and his iron-clad determination that flowed into her. It inspired her every time. He'd arrived home a few minutes ago, but she'd learned he had a routine and it was best not to disturb it so she'd kept on playing. He looked as divine as ever in a blue-and-white checked shirt, navy collared light jumper and the palest of grey chinos.

Before she'd started living at the penthouse, she'd wondered how he managed to coordinate his clothes so well, when his hair always looked slightly unkempt and rumpled. Now she knew. He bought an entire season of clothes from a particular men's store and his cleaning lady hung them in colour groups.

She smiled up at him. 'Before I forget, Carol rang to say she's home and she suggested dinner soon.'

'Let me know your roster and I'll call her later.'

Delicious surprise flowed through her that he wanted her to meet the woman who'd been more of a mother to him than his own and she hugged it close. 'Will do. You're back early.'

He dropped a kiss onto her head. 'And you're not studying.'

'Your powers of deduction amaze me, Watson.'

He smiled gently. 'You're rolling your eyes at me.'

How did he know that? 'No, I'm not.'

His fingers played with her hair. 'You're also a hopeless liar, Hayley. I can hear it in your voice. Bad day?'

It had been an awful day, starting with a young motorcyclist who'd wrapped himself around a tree and almost bled to death on the table, and it had ended with what should have been a straightforward division of adhesions, but when she'd opened up the patient's peritoneum it had been riddled with cancer. She'd immediately closed up, stitching each layer with great care, and two hours later had broken the bad news that the woman had only weeks to live. After all of that she'd had her second appointment with the hypnotherapist. She hadn't wanted to go to the first appointment, but Tom had pushed and chivvied and walked her there to make sure she'd followed through on her promise. It hadn't been the ordeal she'd expected and today's return visit had left her feeling oddly light inside. She kept rubbing her chest, expecting the familiar heavy weight to return.

While she'd been living with Tom, she'd got used to talking about her day with him, as well as chatting about all sorts of things from medicine to politics and books. Their taste in books was poles apart, but she didn't care because the discussions that stemmed from their differences was invigorating. She hadn't felt this alive or shared her thoughts like this with a friend in...

Never as an adult.

Or as a teenager. When Amy died, she'd stopped sharing her thoughts with others and she'd never experienced a strong connection with anyone since, but now with Tom, it felt...right.

Her arm crossed her chest as she placed her hand on top of his. 'It was a seriously lousy day, but how did you know?'

'You're playing the piano.'

She laughed. 'I've been known to play the piano after a good day.'

He raised his brows and put his hands on the piano stool, feeling for the edges. She moved along, creating some space, and he sat down next to her. His hand pressed on her thigh and a tingle shot through her.

'Just as I thought.' He smiled at her. 'You're wearing what I assume are old and faded tracksuit pants. They're your comfort clothes.'

She stared at him, aghast that he'd worked that out about her. She only wore them because he couldn't see how tatty they were. 'How do you even know I own tracksuit pants?'

He laughed. 'You're chronically untidy, Hayley, and I tripped over them once in the bedroom.'

'Oh, hell, I'm sorry.' Learning to share a house with someone after years of living alone was one thing. Sharing with a blind man was something else entirely. 'I can move out if it's not working.'

Please say no.

He squeezed her thigh. 'My offer stands, but I think I've worked out the reason you're still single.'

His teasing made her smile. 'Your logic is flawed. If I'm single due to being messy, how come you're single when you're a neat-freak?'

'I tried living with a woman once, but the relationship got in the way of what I wanted to achieve and I can't see that ever changing. What's your excuse?'

She blinked at his unexpected reply. He wasn't known for volunteering that sort of information about himself and his question to her caught her unprepared. 'I don't think I'm the sort of person who falls in love.'

Her heart suddenly rolled over and she rubbed her chest at the ache.

'I knew you were a sensible woman.'

His words circled her, adding to the ache and bringing with them an unaccountable sadness that swamped her. She tried to shrug it away but it wouldn't leave. She sighed as confusion added to the mix. 'That's me. Pragmatic and sensible.'

He leaned in, his hand seeking her cheek, and then he kissed her gently. 'Talking of sensible, while you're here, can you please try and pick up and put things where they belong so I don't break a leg?'

She bit her lip. It was incredibly generous of him but she was compelled to tell him about the phone call she'd received earlier in the day. 'I spoke to the insurance assessor today and although the job's been approved, the problem is finding tradesmen because they're swamped with work.' She took in a deep breath. 'It could be a month or longer.'

He didn't say anything and for a moment she thought she read regret on his face. Regret that he'd offered so quickly that she should stay for as long as it took to fix her house. Then he nudged her arm with his. 'At the rate you're going I'll have just got you house-trained and it will be time for you to leave.'

'Hey.' Indignation flowed through her on the back of relief. 'I'm not that bad.'

This time he rolled his eyes. 'Even Gladys commented on the spare room mess.'

'Gladys complains about everything.'

'True, but I knew her before I went blind and I know she cleans everything to within an inch of its life so I'm keeping her.'

She pondered that. Did Tom think people would take advantage of his lack of sight? He fought the limitations of his blindness every single second of every single day and his quest for independence was almost a religion. Apart from her lapses in tidiness, she'd quickly learned to unobtrusively assist him only when it was absolutely necessary and that usually only happened when they were out. When they were home, she forgot he was blind—to her he was just Tom.

Smart, gorgeous, wickedly ironic and with a caring streak a mile wide—not that he'd admit it. He made her feel special, cared for and safe. Very safe. These last ten days, sharing his apartment and living with him, had been the best ten days of her life. She loved being here with him.

You love him.

No. That's not possible. I don't fall in love. We're good friends. Mates.

You're way more than that and you know it. The empty space around your heart's vanished. It's why you just felt so sad when he called you sensible. It's why the thought of moving out of here hurts.

Oh, hell, she loved him.

Her breath caught in her throat as the reality hit her so hard she almost swayed. How had it happened? How had she fallen in love? What she and Tom shared was supposed to be sex and friendship, and falling in love was never part of the deal. He was adamant he didn't want a relationship and it had never even crossed her radar as something to be cautious of because she'd never given her heart to anyone. When Amy had died, she'd closed down to avoid any more hurt. She specialised in keeping things light with everyone and maintaining distance. She'd never anticipated falling in love.

But it had sneaked up on her so slowly she hadn't even realised it was happening.

Are you sure it's not just lust?

But she knew it was way beyond that. The feeling was so different from the hot, burning need she experienced every time they had sex. No, this was like the steady warmth from an Aga stove—it eddied around her in a blanket of comfort and filled her with an all-encompassing happiness that made her smile all the time.

His right hand started playing the top notes of 'Heart and Soul' and she automatically started playing the bass to the well-known piece. It triggered a memory, but it didn't douse her with pain like it might have done once. 'I used to play this with Amy.'

'It's all I can play.' He gave her a gentle smile, reached for her right hand and squeezed it.

Her heart swelled in a rush and she glanced at his handsome profile. Did he love her? Had love slowly arrived with him as well?

The relationship got in the way of what I wanted to achieve.

That was when he was living a different life. He comes home early from work when he knows you're home.

That he cared for her she was in no doubt.

Caring was part of love.

Was the gap between caring and love so very big? She hoped not.

She kept playing the continuous loop with one hand while her other snuggled in his, adoring their close connection and wanting to build on it. Build a future. 'Why do you have such a beautiful grand piano if you don't play?'

His hand slowed on the keys. 'When you grow up with nothing, once you have money you tend to spend it on things the inner child was deprived of.'

'An expensive home, a fast car and a piano?'

'Got it in one.'

'Anything else?' She had an overwhelming need to know much more about the man she loved.

His head tilted in thought. 'I'd always planned on getting a dog, but I was never home enough.'

'And that's why you didn't get around to piano lessons?'

'Running The Harbour's neurosurgery department didn't leave me with any time. I was never home.'

She suddenly had a brilliant idea. 'So learn now.'

He stopped playing altogether and let go of her hand, his body bristling with intransigent tension. 'Why? Because once the lecture series is over I'm unemployed and will have all the time in the world?'

'No.' She held her voice steady, refusing to fall into his

argument trap. 'Look, I know you're not certain what's coming next or what you want to do and that's unsettling, but if learning the piano is something you've always wanted to do, it won't happen if you don't make it a priority.'

Shoving himself to his feet, he caught the edge of the piano with his hip as he moved away. He swore and rubbed the bruised skin with his hand. 'Learning to live blind is my priority. That's my focus for the coming year.'

She bit off her automatic 'Are you okay?', saying instead, 'It's been your priority and it's paid off in spades. You're already doing amazingly well. Do you really need to take off another year?'

He made a strangled sound. 'When I can use echolocation exclusively and walk without a cane, *that* will be doing amazingly well.'

His derisive expression ripped through her and she chewed her lip, feeling anxious for him. 'Tom, that's an admirable goal, but is it realistic?'

Anger scored his face. 'Of course it bloody is.'

She rose to her feet and ran her hand along his arm, wanting to soothe. 'If you hate the cane so much, why not think about a guide dog?'

'No.'

He shook her arm away, his expression full of hurt. It was like she'd just mortally offended him.

'Tom, I was only trying to—'

He held up his hand. 'Look, we've both got work to do before dinner. You need to study and I have to convert my notes into braille for my final few lectures. I'll leave you to it.'

He turned and walked away from her, the action as

sharp and loud as a door being slammed in her face. Her heart took the hit, and the deep purple stain of a bruise spread out across it.

CHAPTER TEN

'BLOODY bow tie. I could never tie the damn things when I could see. Why does the vice chancellor's dinner have to be formal?'

Tom almost flung the offending piece of silk onto the floor, but restrained himself because Hayley was sitting on the bed. There was something about her that made him want to control his frustration, which was odd because all his life he'd never experienced the urge to do that. Tonight it was hard to control because he needed to go to this dinner, but a large crowd in a noisy room meant a tough night for him.

Although he'd never admit it out loud, the fact Hayley had accepted his invitation to be his guest had mitigated some of his concerns about attending. She, unlike most people, had the knack of knowing when he needed the hated assistance and when he didn't. Well, most of the time. She'd both crossed the line and shocked him when she'd suggested a guide dog. He'd thought she understood how important it was to him that he be totally independent.

Now, under the thread of his controlled anxiety about the evening was a simmer of anticipation. Hayley was fun to be with and her presence would temper any boring speeches that might be part of the event, given that Guy

Laurent was retiring. Tom could remember attending lectures given by 'The Prof' when he'd been a med student and Parkes wouldn't be quite the same without him.

'It's a formal affair because a hundred and fifty years ago, when the first dinner was held, the tuxedo was de rigueur and you would have had a valet to dress you,' Hayley said. 'Besides, some traditions are worth holding on to. Plus, it fits in with Parkes's amazing sandstone cloisters and the dining room with its high vaulted ceiling.'

She sounded almost wistful and the rustle of material as she stood up evoked a bygone era. 'But most importantly…' she gave a wicked laugh '…it makes all the men look as sexy as hell.'

'So you plan on scoping out the talent this evening, do you?' He'd intended the words to come out as joke, but they sounded unexpectedly tight and if they were to be awarded a colour, it would have been green.

'Absolutely.'

Her smoky voice rode on top of a cloud of musky sandalwood scent, which wrapped around him as she stepped in close. The deeper and sexier evening fragrance was a delicious assault on his nostrils and in stark contrast to her more innocent summer-fresh scent of flowers with a citrus tang. His pulse quickened.

Hayley's fingers brushed his neck as she pulled the material of the tie toward her and he moved with it, his lips meeting hers in a kiss she immediately deepened.

His arms instantly wrapped around her waist and he matched the kiss, wanting nothing more than to tear whatever she was wearing off her and follow the trail of that intoxicating scent. He broke off the kiss, the thought of staying in with Hayley burning strong. 'We could just stay home.'

'And waste my *one* opportunity of the year to get out of scrubs and wear a dress? I don't think so.'

Her knuckles brushed his skin as her fingers tied and tugged at the bow tie. 'There you go. Now you're complete. You look all dark and decadent, like a man of mystery.'

'And what do you look like?' His hands settled on her hips, and then dropped lower, fisting into an ocean of soft, filmy material he couldn't name. He then trailed upwards, across a tight fitted bodice that outlined the nip of her waist and the swell of her breasts and then his fingers touched skin. Warm, smooth skin that dipped and rose until his fingers nestled between her breasts. He swallowed hard and his voice came out hoarse. 'Strapless?'

She laughed. 'Totally strapless. It's black with a band of white satin at the top of the bodice so I match you in black and white.'

An ache unlike anything he'd ever experienced took hold of him. 'I wish I could see you.'

She caught his hands and placed one on her back and one on her chest and her voice came out soft and low. 'You've already seen more of me than I've ever shown anyone.'

Her words vibrated deep down inside him before echoing back and he realised that over the last few weeks he'd shared more about himself with her than he'd ever shared with any other person. He hadn't intended that to happen—it just had. She'd slipped into his life and into his home with an ease that stunned him. Since arriving back in Sydney, his home had been his sanctuary from the world—the one place he could really relax. He'd thought Hayley would damage that and he'd be spending more time at work, but instead she'd made his home even more of a refuge. Just lately he'd even had moments of wondering what it might be like if she stayed.

Great sex every night.

Huh! In your dreams. If you ask her to stay it will turn into your worst nightmare with her thinking white dresses, redecorating and babies.

Children?

The thought rolled around in his head with burgeoning roots, eagerly trying to find a place to settle. A slight tremor of panic ruffled his equilibrium.

His watch beeped seven o'clock, interrupting his anomalous daydream and bringing him firmly back to the present. 'I told Jared we'd get a taxi because he had a party to go to so we'd better head downstairs. Are you ready to go?'

She slid her arm along his. 'I'm all yours.'

Hayley watched Tom walking across the empty dance floor on his way back to their table, his shoulders square and his face stern, but she knew it was from concentration, not ill-humour. He'd been tense when they'd arrived earlier in the evening, but she'd quietly given him the layout of the room and once they'd taken their seats for dinner, he'd relaxed. It had been Tom, with his humour and entertaining stories, who had been the glue at their table, setting everyone at ease and making her laugh along with the rest of the guests. She could hardly believe she'd thought him taciturn and rude when she'd first met him.

Tonight had been pretty much perfect. Tom had kept his arm draped casually over the back of her chair for most of the evening and more than once his fingers had caressed her bare shoulders in a public display of affection she hadn't ever expected in her wildest dreams. She hugged it to herself as a sign that perhaps she wasn't the only one falling in love.

Tom stopped just short of the table. 'Hayley?'

She rose and crossed to him. 'Right here. You've said your farewells to Guy?'

He nodded. 'He's pretty excited about his retirement and takes off for France next week.'

'Lucky Guy.'

He groaned at the play on words. 'I think he's heard that a lot this evening. Are you ready to leave?'

'Sure, I'll just grab my things.' She took five short steps to the chair, picked up her evening bag and wrap, and when she turned back Tom was in conversation with Richard Hewitson, the dean of the school of medicine. She'd chatted to him earlier in the evening.

He nodded at her in recognition. 'I was just asking Tom if he'd made up his mind.'

'Oh?' Hayley had no idea what Richard meant and she glanced at Tom for a clue, but his face was expressionless except for a line of tension along his jaw.

Richard smiled. 'Guy's retirement has opened up a spot in the faculty and Tom would bring new vigour to the position, but he's holding out on us. It would be great if you could convince him to join us on staff.'

Joy for Tom rocked through her and she opened her mouth to speak but Tom got in first.

'Richard…' His voice had the 'don't push me' tone, which anyone who knew him well would recognise. 'I'll be in touch.'

Richard shook Tom's hand, completely missing the warning. 'Looking forward to it, but don't wait too long.' He then extended his hand to Hayley. 'Lovely to meet you and I hope we'll all be seeing a lot more of each other.'

She quickly murmured her goodbyes and caught up

with Tom, who'd already started walking in the direction of the exit with a white-knuckled grip on his cane.

Tom needed to move. He needed to walk off his anger at Richard. The cool outside air hit him the moment he stepped out the door and although he couldn't see the bare jacaranda trees he remembered how they cast long shadows against the sandstone buildings. As a student he'd often sat in the quad, staring at the clock tower, not quite believing that he'd come so far from Derrybrook and was studying in such hallowed halls. He'd also felt inspired by the sight just before exams and he'd missed his time at university when he'd qualified. But that had been years ago and he wasn't ready to come back. He couldn't believe the dean had mentioned the job to Hayley with the sole intent of forcing him to make a decision quickly.

Hayley's feet slowed. 'Did you call a taxi?'

'No.' His raw and restless energy surged. 'It's not far. Can you walk home in your shoes?'

'They're high but comfortable but I won't be striding out.' Her hand touched his elbow. 'Which way do we go?'

He turned forty-five degrees and started walking. 'Straight down The Avenue, through Graffiti Pass—'

'Is it lit at night?'

'Yes. And then out onto the main road. It's only five minutes from there.'

'That will be handy if you decide to take the job.'

He swung his cane in wide arcs, knowing this route home well. 'I won't be taking it.'

'Why not?'

He heard her surprise and it bit him. 'Because it's beneath me.'

'You're going to have to explain that to me.'

'You think I should take a job teaching anatomy and physiology to first-year medical students?'

'You'd be really good at it.'

'I'd hate it.' He stabbed the ground with his cane. 'I was a neurosurgeon, for God's sake. I should be lecturing in neurology at the very least.'

'Guy lectured in other areas. Perhaps this is just a starting position.' Her mild tone meant she was working hard not to sound cross. 'Look at the positives. It's a professorship at a prestigious university connected to one of the world's best teaching hospitals. It would open up all sorts of opportunities for you. Given that you can no longer operate, this is about as perfect as it gets.'

He railed against her common-sense words. 'It isn't bloody perfect. It's settling.' He stopped suddenly, his anger having taken over so much that he'd forgotten to count steps and he had no clue where he was.

As if she could read his thoughts Hayley said, 'Graffiti Pass. Four steps down.'

'I know.' He ground out the words, cross with himself and furious at the world.

'Of course you do.' Her voice softened. 'Tom, let's just walk and we can talk about this when we get home.'

'Let's not.' He moved away from her, tapping down the four steps, and continued into the tunnel, hearing the echo of Hayley's steps behind him. Then he heard the sound of running feet. He stopped because the sound was bouncing off the concrete walls and he wasn't certain if the running was coming from behind him or in front of him. He moved to the side.

The noise got louder and the next moment pain exploded in his gut and then in his shoulder. He tumbled backwards and as he hit the wet and gritty floor of the tunnel, he realised he'd just been punched and pushed.

'Hey!' Hayley's yell reverberated around him.

The running feet stalled for a moment and then

Hayley's scream tore through him like a jagged knife. Fear poured through him, burning like acid. Was she hurt? Had she been knifed? Had she been dragged off?

He pushed himself to his knees, primal fear driving him. He had to help her. Protect her. 'Hayley!'

No one replied. All he could hear were the echoes of the running feet being joined by other, sharper echoes. Shock rendered his fledgling echolocation inadequate and he stretched out his hand, trying to find his cane. He needed the damn thing more than ever. Needed it to help Hayley. Something sharp sliced into his hand, but he didn't care, he kept on feeling, spreading his hands over what was probably broken glass in an ever-increasing circle, but all he could feel was the floor of the tunnel.

You can't protect her. You can't even find a bloody cane.

The thought barrelled into him hard and fast, sucking his breath from his lungs and drenching him in cold sweat.

You're totally useless to her.

Hayley dabbed the cuts on Tom's hand with antiseptic and tried to infuse some lightness into her voice after the shock of seeing him being pushed to the ground. He'd been eerily quiet from the moment she'd handed him his cane in the underpass and, despite having had a shower and a finger of whisky, he still seemed detached and a million miles away from her. Shock could do that.

'The police say it's unlikely they'll catch whoever snatched my bag, but at least the bastard only got a cheap phone with a crappy ringtone and ten dollars.'

Tom didn't reply. She put a plaster over the deepest cut and then kissed his hand. 'I've removed all the gravel so they should heal up fast.'

'Thank you.' A muscle twitched under his left eye as he put his hands in his lap. 'I should never have suggested we walk home.'

'We walk most places. It's one of the things I love about inner-city living.' She rose and walked around the table, putting her hands on his shoulders and dropping her head onto his. 'What happened tonight was not your fault. It was just one of those things. The underpass was well lit and there's security all over the campus. I think this guy just made a split-second decision.'

He gave a snort of derision. 'Because I was blind.'

The bitterness in his voice dried her mouth. 'Because we were in evening dress and we looked rich.' She wanted him to put his hand up and touch her cheek, like he often did, but he sat perfectly still like he was carved out of stone and she could feel her reassurances just sliding off him.

She walked around and picked up his hands and then leaned in, pressing her lips to his forehead. 'I'm just glad you weren't seriously hurt. It's really late so let's go to bed. Tomorrow's a new day.'

He shook his head. 'You go.'

A skitter of unease shot through her. Not once in all their time together had he ever said no to her when she'd suggested they go to bed, no matter the time of day or night. 'I sleep better with you when it's dark.' She snuggled onto his lap and ran her finger along his lips. 'Not that I intend to go to sleep right away.'

He started to rise, effectively tipping her off his lap. 'You can't depend on me to sleep, Hayley. You can't depend on me for anything.'

His words carried the sting of a slap and her heart cramped. 'Tom, what's going on?'

He'd walked over to the couch and gripped the back

with his hand. 'You could have been seriously hurt tonight and I couldn't do a damn thing to stop it.'

His feelings mirrored hers. 'I saw you get pushed to the ground and I couldn't do a damn thing to stop it either. I agree it was horrible.'

He swung back toward her, the movement stiff. 'You're deliberately being obtuse. If I'd been able to see, I would have made sure you were protected.'

She crossed the room and put her arms around him, wanting to disabuse him of the thought. 'You don't know that for a fact. It all happened so fast and every day the paper's full of assaults on sighted people who can't defend themselves or the people they're with during an attack.' She stroked his face. 'But I love that you wanted to protect me.'

'Of course I want to protect you.'

His granite expression had softened and his quietly spoken words lined up perfectly with all the care and concern he'd showered her with over recent weeks.

He's made the leap too. He loves you.

Sheer joy expanded her heart so much she almost cried and she kissed him deeply. Then the words she'd been saying silently to herself for days slipped out. 'I love you, Tom.'

For a tiny moment panic closed her throat. Had she misconstrued his words? But Tom didn't stiffen or pull away. Instead, he brought his hand up to her hair and caressed it gently before breathing in deeply as if he was inhaling part of her to keep.

He kissed her hair. 'My Hayley.'

My Hayley. She was his. She rested her head on his shoulder and gave a blissful sigh, knowing that he loved her and they belonged together. The future rolled out in front of her like a magic carpet—the two of them together and sharing life's journey. She'd never known such happiness and it swam through her, warming her until she was bathed in a rosy glow.

He slowly brought his hands to rest on her arms and then he set her apart from him. 'I think it's best if you move out tomorrow.'

Her knees sagged in shock and her chest refused to move. She scanned his face but couldn't read it. Of all the words she'd expected him to say, those weren't among them. 'You…you want me to leave?'

He gave a curt nod, his expression blank. 'It's been fun, Hayley, but it's over.'

A million thoughts zoomed around in her head but none of them fully formed because all the foundations had been stripped away. 'I don't understand. You just said "my Hayley". I thought you loved me.'

'Love's got nothing to do with it.' He sounded ragged and worn out. 'You and I are never going to work.'

A surge of hope pushed her shock aside momentarily and she sought to clarify his words. 'But you do love me?'

'I don't know.' He ran his hand through his chocolate-noir hair and his face sagged, making his five o'clock shadow darker than ever. 'Love wasn't in my house when I was growing up, and the lack of it ruined my mother's life. Being with someone isn't something I've ever wanted, and being with you is the closest I've ever come to that.'

I don't know. She tried not to let his words wound and instead concentrated on trying to hear what he was really saying. 'So you've thought about us being together in the future?'

'Occasionally.'

Hope shot up. *That's better than never. Build on that.* 'When you thought about us, what were we doing?'

A mellow smile softened his expression but then his

mouth hardened. 'There's no point talking about this, Hayley. I've never wanted to be in a relationship and added to that I'm now blind. Tonight just made everything more clear to me and ably demonstrated that I can't protect you, let alone children.'

She gasped, totally stunned as her heart did somersaults. 'You've thought about us having children?'

His bladed cheeks sharpened. 'Only how they'd be in danger with me and I wouldn't be able to be a proper father and take care of them.' His fist slammed into his palm with a slap. 'Hell, they could walk out the door and I wouldn't know they'd gone. We wouldn't work, Hayley.'

She grabbed his hands—desperate to connect with him and show him that they did have a future. A future he'd glimpsed but was now rejecting. 'We can make it work. Together we're a team and we complement each other, you know that. It's what we've been doing these last few weeks.'

She tried to think of an example but her brain was still recovering from the shock of him asking her to leave. She grabbed on to the first thought that floated past. 'You know I'm hopeless at computer stuff and you're sensational at it, so you can teach them all the technology and I'll—'

'Do everything else?' His brow shot up in a sardonic tilt as he pulled his hands away and strode across the room.

Desperation made words flood out of her. 'We'd get help. That's what housekeepers and nannies are for.' She thought of her mother and smiled. 'And grandmothers.'

He gave a harsh laugh that sliced through the air, leaving a chill in its wake. 'I can't contribute one of those.'

She refused to let him wallow in self-pity. 'You're *not* without family, Tom. Carol would love to help and Jared can be the bachelor uncle who lets the kids stay up all night watching inappropriate films and eating too much chocolate.'

He shook his head. 'Stop dreaming, Hayley. It would all fall apart.'

'No, it won't.'

'Yes, it will.'

She wanted to shake him free of this crazy notion. 'It would only happen because you believe it will.'

'This is nothing to do with believing and everything to do with knowing.' His yelled words settled over them like a shroud. 'I'm a realist, Hayley.'

Her heart hammered hard and fast as she fought for their future. 'No, this isn't realism. This is you being a fool, and that's exactly what you'll be if you walk away from what *will* be a wonderful and amazing life together.'

He didn't respond and her shoulders slumped. 'Tom, this makes no sense.'

'It makes all the sense in the world.' His shoulders rolled back in a familiar action of determination. 'I'm doing you a favour. Ending it now will save us long-term pain. You'd only end up resenting me and resenting the blindness. Hell, I resent it. It will tear us apart and then you'll leave, like everyone else.'

Her heart spasmed for him. How could she argue against a childhood of abandonment?

With the truth. 'I don't care that you're blind. To me you're just Tom, the most giving and caring man I've ever had the fortune to meet. You're the man I love and I won't ever leave you.'

'You say that now, but everyone does.' He flinched, the tremor moving across his shoulders and ricocheting down his legs. 'This is the reason I've stayed single and now that I'm blind it's even more important. You have no idea what it was like for me tonight in that underpass and

I'm never allowing myself to feel that vulnerable again. I've never depended on anyone and I'm not about to start.'

She wanted to scream and rage at him, but she knew he'd just tune her out completely. 'Tom, I have twenty-twenty vision and I depend on you in so many ways, big and small. Without you, I'd still be chronically exhausted, but you forced me to deal with my PTSD and I'm making progress. There's nothing wrong with needing people. No one is completely independent of others and if they are, well, it's a sad life and they're not happy.'

He turned slowly and she saw that the warm glow that had been living in his eyes for a few weeks had now vanished. A knife-sharp pain tore through her heart and she knew right there and then that she'd lost the argument.

Lost him.

'You don't want to fight for us, do you?'

'I'm sorry.' He walked toward the spare room, 'I'll sleep here tonight and Jared can help you move tomorrow. Have a good life, Hayley.' He closed the door softly behind him.

'I never took you for a coward, Tom Jordan,' she yelled as she hurled a couch cushion at the door and then watched it fall with a quiet thud to the floor. Her shaking legs gave way completely and she collapsed onto the couch, her breath coming in ragged runs. For years she'd held herself apart from people, but Tom had slipped under her guard and into her heart, digging in for the long haul and making her dream.

Now he'd killed the dream, but the love stayed on, lamenting what might have been.

She buried her face in her hands and silently wept.

CHAPTER ELEVEN

EVIE arrived at Pete's, glanced around and sighed. She couldn't see Lexi anywhere. Her sister had texted her twice in the last hour, reminding her to meet her here, and now Evie had not only arrived but arrived on time and Lexi was nowhere to be seen.

She headed toward the bar, but stalled at a table tucked away in a corner. 'Hayley?'

'That's me.'

Even in the mood lighting of the bar, Evie could see the registrar's drawn expression and sorrow-filled eyes. Hayley wasn't a regular at Pete's—in fact, she was a bit of a loner, although The Harbour gossip mill had her linked with Tom Jordan but no one seemed to know too much about it. The fact she was sitting here meant something was up. 'May I join you?'

Hayley sighed and pushed out an adjacent chair. 'Sure.'

Evie noticed Hayley was drinking mineral water and she called over to the bar. 'Hey, Pete, I'm off the clock so can you please bring me one of your Harbour Specials?'

Pete gave her a wave. 'Anything for you, Dr Lockheart.'

Evie returned the wave and sat down. 'Are you okay? You look absolutely wiped.'

Hayley fiddled with a coaster. 'It's been a long day on all fronts.'

'Of course. Sorry, I should have realised.' Earlier in the day, a twenty-three-year-old had wrapped his car around a pole, injuring himself and his three passengers. All available staff had been called in and she knew that Finn and Hayley had been in Theatre most of the day, dealing with the emergency as well as trying to clear their delayed surgical list. 'Has Finn Kennedy been giving you hell?'

'I wish.' Hayley leaned back and laughed, but the sound was neither happy nor ironic. 'Actually, I got a rare compliment from Mr Kennedy today.'

'A compliment?' Evie couldn't hide her astonishment and yet at the same time she was unaccountably happy that Finn had been able to voice praise. She knew he found expressing any sort of positive emotion incredibly difficult.

'There you go, Evie, a Harbour Special, as requested.' Pete put the glass of beer down with a grin and returned to the bar.

Hayley stirred her mineral water with her straw and gave a half-smile. 'You know our chief of surgery, Evie. He's taciturn and a man of few words, but after we'd patched a frayed femoral artery courtesy of an impacted steering column, he said, "When you qualify we'd consider an application from you."'

That's so Finn. 'You know it means he wants you working here as a consultant and part of his team.' She raised her glass. 'Congratulations, Hayley.'

'Thanks.' She picked up her glass and clinked it against Evie's, but the action lacked enthusiasm.

'You don't sound very thrilled.' Evie realised she didn't know much at all about Hayley except that she was always obliging when the ER requested a surgical consult and she hadn't shied away from the tough decisions or the hard asks. 'You're not long back from the UK, are you? Were you planning on going back or working somewhere else in Oz?'

Hayley shook her head and compressed her lips. 'No. My heart was set on settling down in Sydney, here, in fact, but—' Hayley's phone honked like a ferry horn and she glanced down at the liquid display and sighed. 'Sorry, Evie, I'm on call and that's Mia McKenzie from ER. Sounds like it's a good night for you to be off duty and out of there. Enjoy yourself.' She rose and hurried out the door.

Evie realised that once again Hayley had been friendly and yet had managed not to give out much information about herself at all. While they'd been talking, Pete's had filled up but there was still no sign of Lexi and with the first few sips of the beer warming her veins, Evie had no desire to sit on her own. She stood up, looking for someone from The Harbour, but none of the chattering groups in the deep and comfy booths were people she knew. Picking up her drink, she headed to the bar to chat with Pete, who was always entertaining, but stopped short a few steps away, instantly recognising the taut set of broad shoulders and long legs that were wound around a bar-stool.

Finn.

She swallowed hard.

Sure, they saw each other at work but there was always a patient and a team of staff between them. The last occasion they'd been alone together had been when time had stood still. He'd leaned into her and she'd pressed herself against his warm, broad back, wanting nothing more than to stay there for ever. Her surge of feelings for him then had been so unexpected that they'd both terrified her and filled her with a hope she'd never dared to dream of. Then he'd lurched away from her, to this very bar, and straight into the arms of another woman.

She didn't want to relive *that* particular memory of him flirting with the OR nurse when he'd known that she was still in the bar with a full view of what he was doing. Deliberately hurting her.

She swayed slightly. Seeing him at work was one thing—she didn't have a choice there, but she did have a choice now. She didn't have to see him socially.

'Something wrong with your drink, Evie?' Pete enquired as he flung a bar towel over his shoulder.

Finn immediately turned around, his vivid blue gaze torching her. She hated that she stood stock-still like a rabbit caught in headlights. Hated that she hadn't moved half a second earlier before Pete had seen her. Before Finn had seen her.

Put on your mask.

She tilted her chin and strode toward the bar, standing next to the seated Finn. 'All alone tonight?'

'Not any longer.' He raised his glass of malt whisky to her and his eyes simmered with a swirl of caged emotions, none of which held form long enough to be named.

She gulped her drink as she felt herself being pulled in by them. 'Oh, I'm not staying.'

'No?'

She slammed the empty glass down on the long counter. 'No. I make it a rule not to spend any time with people who are immersed in self-destruction.'

His right brow lifted. 'That rules out all the interesting people. Does it feel good, living a vanilla life, Evie?'

Anger drove caution to the wind and lifted the mask on her heart. 'Does it feel good rejecting everyone around you who cares, Finn?'

His fingers tightened around his glass and he tossed back his drink. 'Do-gooders don't interest me.'

His words slashed her, breaking open her barely sealed emotions, and a rush of hurt spouted like a geyser. 'In that case you can hope that Suzy Carpenter will be along soon to keep you company.'

His blue eyes narrowed. 'I suppose I can.' He tapped the edge of his glass. 'Pete, give us another one.'

Nausea gripped Evie at his brutal dismissal. She grabbed her bag off the bar and strode toward the door, no longer caring if Lexi was going to arrive or not. She had to leave. Had to get out before she threw up and added to her utter humiliation. Pulling open the heavy wooden door, she stepped out into the night and gulped in a lungful of cool evening air.

Why had she been so foolish? Why? What was it about Finn that made her act so out of character? She was always in control and yet, with a few poorly chosen words, she'd just exposed her jumbled feelings for him. Feelings that she'd wanted to keep hidden because telling a man who was so emotionally shut down that she cared was like putting a match to an incendiary bomb. The ensuing explosion only hurt her.

Not Finn.

No, Finn hadn't been affected at all. He'd read her face, he'd heard her words, and he'd instantly rejected them and her. There had been no ambiguity. He had no feelings for her and he'd made that abundantly clear.

Tom was running late and the day had been quickly going downhill from the moment he'd overslept. The irony that he'd been wide awake at four a.m. wasn't lost on him.

'Jared? Where the hell are my keys?'

'You always leave your keys in the dish by the door.'

'And if they were there, would I be asking you?'

Jared's heavy footfalls headed toward the door. 'I dunno. You've been grumpy and losing things ever since Hayley's house got finished. It's kinda funny because when she was living here you complained that her mess made it hard for you but now everything's all neat again you're losing more stuff than ever.'

Jared's words cut too close to the bone to be comfortable. It was true, his concentration had been all over the place since he'd asked Hayley to leave, but no way in hell was he admitting to it. 'I'll have you know that she lost more things than I ever did.'

Jared snorted. 'Yeah, right. Hey, Tom, did you drink a lot last night?'

Was a bottle of merlot and a whisky chaser a lot? 'Why?'

'Because…' Jared laughed '…I've found your keys in the fruit basket.'

Damn it, how had he done that?

The same way you put your wallet in the fridge. You were thinking about Hayley.

Tom banished the unwanted thought and snapped his hand out for the needed items. 'Thanks. Let's go. Now. The last thing I need is smart-arse late jokes from one hundred and twenty med students.' He slung his computer satchel over his chest, flicked out his cane and headed toward the lifts.

'Excuse me.'

An accented and unknown voice hailed Tom as he prepared to leave the lecture hall. He sighed. The day had been a long one. The whole damn week had been excruciatingly long without Hayley in it, but finally it was Friday and he'd survived the first week without her. He'd survive the next and the one after that and the one after that, stretching well into the future.

He hated that he'd hurt her but, no matter what she believed, he knew he'd made the right decision. With each passing week she'd come to realise that he'd actually freed her.

So, if it was the right decision, why does it feel like hell?

'Mr Jordan?'

The foreign accent reminded him he was supposed to reply. 'Yes?'

'I'm Akim Deng, medical student, and I follow your lectures with most great interest.'

Tom put out his hand on hearing the formal sentence structure so often used by people where English was a second or subsequent language. 'Where are you from, Akim?'

'Blacktown.'

Tom smiled. The western suburbs continued to be a melting pot of nationalities, just like it had been when he'd been a kid. 'I used to live near there, but I meant where did you live before Blacktown?'

'Oh, I am from the Sudan, but before Australia I lived in Kenya for some years.'

Tom mentally filled in blanks that the 'some years' had most likely been spent in a refugee camp. He knew how hard the struggle out of poverty was and he'd not had to cope with the language barrier. 'How are you finding medical school?'

'I am honoured to be here.'

'I'm sure you'll make the most of your opportunity, then. Good to meet you, Akim.' Feeling that the conversation was over, Tom unfurled his cane.

'Not every teacher is like you.'

Blind? An ex-surgeon? The zip of fury that had lessened in recent weeks roared through him and he worked on keeping the edge out of his voice. 'No. They're not.'

Akim sighed. 'Sadly, no.'

Tom's feet, which had been ready to move, suddenly stilled. 'What do you mean?'

The student hesitated for a moment before saying, 'I do not need to seek help from other students to understand your lectures.'

Shock at the frankness of the student lit a fire under his collegiate support. 'I'm sure my colleagues would be happy to explain things if you're not following their lectures.'

'Often they use the same words over and over, which does not help in understanding.'

Sadly, Tom knew what he meant. Some of the older lecturers had been in the job for years and hadn't realised that the world had changed, students had changed, and lecturing styles needed to keep pace.

'I like how you use examples. It makes the theory real.' Akim's voice filled with appreciation. 'I can picture it all and this helps when I am meeting patients. I can hear your voice and see the pictures in my head. I am now thinking of neurology for my future.'

'Not neurosurgery?' Tom joked. 'I can't have been doing my job very well, then.'

Akim's hand touched his arm. 'Believe me, Mr Jordan, you do your job very well. I am sad your lectures are finishing.'

You're a fantastic teacher, Tom.

Hayley's voice suddenly broke through the barrier he'd imposed on everything to do with her, but as he patched up the breach he found himself fishing in his pocket for a business card, which he held out to Akim. 'Give me a call if you ever need a hand with your studies.'

Akim gasped. 'You are very generous. Are you certain it would not bother you?'

You know, mate, you can call by any time.

How many times had Mick said that to him? Every single time he'd seen him, whether it had been at Mick's house or at school or on the footy field. Mick, who'd freely given so much of himself and by default had provided Tom with everything he needed to achieve and create a positive life. Every patient he'd ever operated on to remove a brain tumour he'd done with Mick in mind.

You can't do that any more.

I bloody know that.

Yeah, but can you see what you can do?

It was like hearing Mick's voice again and right then he knew how he could keep Mick's legacy going. Helping Jared had been done unconsciously. *This* would be different.

He reached out his hand and Akim gripped it. 'The only bother would be if you didn't ask me.'

'In that case, I will not bother you often.'

Tom laughed. 'Sounds like a plan, Akim. I'll talk to you soon.'

On the walk home he thought about Akim and wondered how many other medical students there were whose English was their second language and who might need extra tutorial time. This led to thinking about Jared who'd headed back to finish school after realising that education was the key to improving his life, but still needed a lot of support to achieve his dream. By the time Tom slipped his key into the front door, his head was filled with ideas and excitement churned his gut. He hadn't experienced such a work-related buzz since the accident and for the very first time he could actually see a work future. One that he was driving rather than having it imposed on him. He couldn't wait to share his thoughts and ideas with Hayley.

He stepped into the apartment and, like a punch to the chest, he remembered she'd gone. The piano was silent, her lingering perfume was now only a faint scent, and the clicks of his tongue as he navigated around the apartment reinforced to him that her clutter was long gone.

You asked her to go.

It's for the best.

The first time he'd come home after she'd left he'd expected a rush of relief, but it hadn't come. Neither had it come the next day and with each passing day it continued to be elusive. He didn't understand because he knew he'd made the right decision. Made the right decision for both of them. Love didn't survive what life threw at it. His parents were a perfect example of that.

Mick and Carol had made it work.

Mick wasn't blind.

He dumped his stuff on the table. He'd ring Carol and tell her his ideas. Why hadn't he thought of telling her first anyway, especially as the whole idea had been generated by his connection to Mick? Flicking open his phone, he said, 'Carol.'

It started ringing and then a warm and familiar voice answered. 'Tom! How lovely. I was just about to call you so how's that for timing? I so enjoyed meeting Hayley at dinner the other night.'

A flicker of guilt washed through him that she telephoned him a lot more than he called her. He immediately told her about his idea, rather than talking about Hayley. 'Of course, I have to sell it to Richard Hewitson, but I think I've some bargaining power.'

Carol laughed. 'You've always had that. You were a

star negotiator at fourteen. I was surprised you didn't go into law.' Her voice sobered. 'Mick was so proud of you the day you got your results and we both knew that you could go to uni and do whatever you put your mind to. If he was still with us he'd be thrilled at what you achieved before the accident and even more so about what you're doing now. So what does Hayley think?'

He closed his eyes out of habit and blew out a slow breath. 'I haven't told her.'

'Oh?' The small sound was loaded with a thousand questions.

He rubbed the back of his neck. 'It was never going to be a long-term thing.'

'Why on earth not?'

He sighed, wishing he'd not answered Carol's first question about Hayley. 'You've always known I don't do relationships, Carol, and I especially don't do them now.'

'You're not seriously telling me that you've broken up with her because you're blind?'

Carol's incredulity spun around him, pulling and pushing at him until he felt unsteady on his feet. 'I appreciate your concern, but it's my life.'

'You don't appreciate my concern in the least, Tom,' she snapped, 'so don't give me that nonsense. I know that anything to do with feelings always makes you uncomfortable and sends you into retreat. I've sat back for years watching you bury yourself in work so you can hold everyone who has ever wanted to care for you at bay. I might have only met Hayley once, but I could see the love she has for you clear on her face and how happy she makes you. If you've let her get away then you're not only blind, you're bloody stupid.'

Carol had never spoken to him like that in his life and

he didn't know if he was shocked, angry or both. 'Are you done?'

'No. Do you love her?'

Carol's question, so familiar to Hayley's, hammered him. He hadn't been able to answer it a week ago and he still couldn't. He knew he cared for her, but love? 'How the hell do I know if I do?'

She let out a long and exasperated sigh. 'Do you enjoy being with her?'

'Yes, but—'

'No "buts", Tom. Only "yes" or "no" answers. Is she the last person you think about when you go to sleep at night and the first person you want to see when you wake up?'

He thought of the last week when he'd hardly slept at all because he'd been constantly thinking of Hayley. He answered with a reluctant, 'Yes.'

'Since you broke it off with her, have you felt like you've been wading through mud and going through the motions of living?'

He tugged at his tie, which suddenly seemed to be choking him. 'Yes.'

'Did you think about telling her about your university plans before you rang me?'

Damn it.

'Tom?'

'Yes.'

Carol's excruciating questions continued. 'Does the idea of spending the rest of your life with her scare you?'

He swallowed in relief. Finally, she'd asked a question where the answer didn't feel like it was being hauled up with a piece of his soul. 'Yes, which is why—'

'Tom.' Carol invoked her best schoolteacher tone.

'When you think about *not* spending the rest of your life with her, does it scare you?'

The words sounded innocent enough and his immediate answer to himself was no, but as his mouth went to form the word he heard the clicking sound of a land mine being engaged. Abject fear tore through him, sweat beaded on his brow and he threw off his jacket. The answer ripped through him with the velocity of an exploding bomb.

Yes.

Oh, hell, he loved her. He truly loved her. 'Carol, I love her, but I can't ask her to spend her life with me when I can't offer her what she needs.'

'And what does she need?'

'A man who doesn't need her.'

Carol gave a confused huff. 'Coming from the most logical male I know, that answer makes no sense at all.'

His heart hammered hard and fast and despite feeling like he was being torn in two he admitted his worst fear. 'I found myself depending on her and I've never depended on anyone. Not before I was blind and especially not now. She doesn't need that in her life.'

'No, she needs a man who loves her.' Carol's voice was quiet but the impact of her words was ear-shattering. 'Tom, you've never been in love before and the logical people are the ones who are thrown most by love. It scares you, but know this. With love comes an amazing interdependence that strengthens individual independence. You're stronger with her than you are without her.'

No one is completely independent of others and if they are, well, it's a sad life and they're not happy.

Hayley's words that he'd so quickly discarded were almost identical to Carol's. Carol, who'd shared her life with Mick for twenty-five years and truly knew what love was through good times and through bad.

So does Hayley. Catch up!

He tried to moisten his dry lips with his tongue, but his mouth was parched. 'Carol, I have to go.'

He didn't wait for her reply.

CHAPTER TWELVE

HAYLEY stared up from her computer at the freshly painted plaster and the beautifully renovated decorative cornices, and wished her heart could be restored so easily. Her little cottage glowed from its hailstorm-imposed redecoration, looking like a woman after a complete make-over. She, on the other hand, knew her hair was lank, that her comfort clothes needed a wash and that she looked a total mess. Sadder still, she was having trouble caring.

The irony of it all was that because of her therapy she was actually getting more hours of uninterrupted sleep than she'd had in years, but not even that was enough to remove the black rings from under her eyes or to fill in the hollows in her cheeks. The theatre staff had noticed and Theo had fussed, Evie had tried to draw her out the night she'd tried to forget everything at Pete's, but it was when Finn Kennedy had glanced at her in ER and said, 'You look like hell. Don't let it affect your work,' that she'd known she must have hit rock bottom.

She turned back to her lecture notes. Her personal life may have fallen apart, but the examiners didn't care about that. They expected her to be an expert on all things surgical and anything less meant failing. Her fingers gripped the computer's stylus overly hard. She would not fail. Being rejected by the man she loved was one thing. She wouldn't allow failing to qualify as a surgeon the first time round to add to her humiliation.

You're doing what Tom does.

What?

Burying yourself in work so you don't have to deal with your feelings.

But what was there to deal with? She'd told Tom she loved him. He'd said, 'Goodbye.'

The loud rap of her door knocker made her jump. She wrapped her fleecy hoodie around her, slipped her feet into her sheepskin boots and walked up the hall, still surprised that the floor no longer dipped. The knocker sounded a second time, and impatience vibrated through the house. 'Okay, just a minute.'

She picked up her keys from a bowl by the door—a habit she'd picked up at Tom's. She shook the thought from her brain as she slid the key into the deadlock before pulling the door open. Her mouth gaped, her throat closed and her heart cramped.

'Hello, Hayley.'

Tom's deep voice spun around her as he stood on her front mat, his height and breadth filling the tiny porch. His hair was dishevelled and for the first time ever he wasn't perfectly colour-coordinated. He wore his royal blue scarf with his brown jacket and black pants. More than the usual amount of black stubble covered his cheeks, giving him a rugged and raw look at odds with the urban-chic clothes. A tingle shot through her and she jumped on it, hating that her desire for him still burned despite how much he'd hurt her. It faded away, leaving her feeling raw and wounded.

She crossed her arms to protect herself. 'That's an interesting combination of clothes. I see as part of your insane drive to be totally independent of anyone you've asked Gladys to leave as well?' Hayley's unexpected response to his greeting thundered into Tom, completely discombobulating him. On the drive over, as Jared had excitedly told him about his A in chemistry, Tom had silently been rehearsing everything he planned to say to her. All of it had been predicated on her saying, 'Hello, Tom.'

He breathed in deeply, savouring the scent of the woman he loved, and tried a smile. 'I've been a bit distracted this last week.'

'How interesting for you.'

Her frigid words almost froze the Sydney winter sun. He steadied himself. 'May I come in?'

'Why?'

Her hurt and anger encased him like the metal bars on a cell. *Did you expect this to be easy?* 'I want to talk to you.'

'I'm not sure—' her voice wavered slightly '—that I want to talk to you.'

He heard the squeak of hinges and he shot out his hand, hoping to stop the door from closing. His knuckles hit something soft.

'Ouch.' Her fingers closed around his hand, pushing it away. 'Hell, Tom. First you break my heart and now you want to give me a black eye?'

His gut rolled on guilt and frustration. 'I'm sorry, but I can't bloody see and I thought you were closing the door on me.' He went for contrition. 'You know I'd never intentionally hurt you.'

'I don't know any such thing.'

His heart shuddered at the hardness in her voice and he sighed. 'Fair call. I deserved that. All I'm asking is for ten minutes and after that you can throw me out.'

Please don't.

'Okay.' Her voice sounded utterly resigned as if she didn't have the energy to say no but that talking to him was something she was being forced to endure. 'It's ten steps down the hall.' She didn't offer her arm. 'Stick to the right to avoid the hall table and there are two steps down into the kitchen. The table with chairs is on your left.'

He wanted to sit next to her without a table between them. 'Do you have a couch we could sit on?'

'I don't think so, Tom.'

Undiluted fear scuttled along his veins at her intractable manner and it took all his concentration to walk to the table without stumbling into something.

Soon after that he heard the legs of her chair scraping on the floor and he realised she was sitting adjacent to him. He folded his hands loosely on the table in front of him. Once he'd thought staying at high school was hard. Once he'd thought the battle to rise out of poverty and carve out a name for himself in neurosurgery was hard, and more recently he'd thought learning how to function as a blind person in a sighted world was the hardest thing he'd ever done. But right now, sitting next to the woman he loved, and feeling the waves of her animosity dumping all over him, he knew that all of it—every other struggle he'd ever endured—paled into insignificance. This was the fight of his life.

He felt her stillness next to him and turned to face her, remembering the soft and curvy feel of her. He stuck to his rehearsed script. 'Hayley, this last week's been the longest of my life. I've missed you so much. I've missed your mess, your music, the way you spread-eagle yourself across the bed and how you talk to me so passionately about your work. You filled my apartment with life and when you left, an emptiness moved in. For the first time in my life I've experienced real loneliness.'

'You did ask me to leave and loneliness is easily fixed. Get a dog or ask Jared to move into the spare room. He's good company.'

Her words shredded him like razor wire and he licked his lips. 'Did you miss hearing the bit where I said it was *you* I missed?'

'No.' The word sounded positively breezy. 'I heard you quite clearly.'

This wasn't going anything like he'd planned and in desperation he abandoned his script. 'Hayley, I love you.'

Her gasp of surprise gave him an injection of hope.

'I don't think you do, Tom.'

Her words crashed around him, shattering his dreams. *You're losing her.* He opened his hands palms up in supplication. 'I'm so sorry that I was slow to realise it, but you must believe me when I tell you that I do love you.'

'I think you've confused love with loneliness.' Her chair scraped back. 'I can't be your friend or your back-up girl with benefits any more, Tom. Goodbye.'

Hope spluttered out like a candle starved of oxygen and he almost doubled over from the visceral pain. His arrogance and pride, which had stood him in such good stead in all other aspects of his life, was worth nothing here. It was as if he'd been cut adrift from everything he'd ever known and he was drowning by inches. He felt for his cane, which he'd hung over the back of his chair, and rose. Her scent twirled around him and he knew she was very close. Like a dying man, he grasped at one last straw. If he could just touch her then perhaps that would connect him to her in a way his words had so miserably fallen short. 'Hayley?' He reached out his hand and prayed she'd take it.

Hayley stared at Tom's face, knowing all the contours and planes so well, having gazed at it for hours and traced it with her fingers and her lips. A face that at times could be as expressionless as granite and at other times open and responsive. Right now, it combined desperation with pleading—two emotions she'd not seen on him before. She wanted to believe what he said, believe that he truly loved her, and she wanted to take his hand, but he'd hurt her too much for her to trust him.

I love you, Hayley.

'Tom, I don't understand. A week ago you locked me out of your life because you believed you couldn't protect me and that as a couple we'd fall at the first hurdle. Over the last seven days you haven't regained your sight so how does the fact you think you love me change anything?'

His hand rested in midair, hovering between them with fingers splayed and a slight tremor at the tips. Her hand tingled and her fingers flexed, but she fisted them to keep them under control.

He cleared his throat. 'The thought of spending the rest of my life without you scared me rigid.'

She pushed her hair out of her eyes as her heart sent new rafts of pain through her with every beat. 'So now you love me out of fear? Great, Tom, I think that's worse than telling me to go.'

The tremor in his hand increased and his jaw tensed as if it didn't want to move and allow the words to come out. 'Apart from Mick and Carol, I've essentially been alone my whole life and I've never allowed myself to need anyone because I was so focused on getting out of Derrybrook and staying out. It drove everything I did. Then you wandered into my life and turned it upside down and you opened my heart to knowing what I'd been missing all these years. Suddenly I wanted all things I'd believed I'd never have. A woman who loved me. A family.' His voice cracked. 'The night in the tunnel when I thought you'd been hurt and I couldn't do a thing to help you terrified me. I never wanted to feel like that again and I asked you to go. I'm beyond sorry.'

She bit her lip against his sorrow, trying to stand firm until she knew exactly what he was really saying. 'Sorry for what?'

His other hand ploughed through his hair as pain scored his face. 'For retreating into a lifelong habit of locking people out and focusing on work. You're right. I try to be insanely independent and losing my sight has only made me worse. It took meeting you to show me how wrong that choice is.'

Her hurting heart hiccoughed. *Be careful.* But her arm lifted and she passively slid her fingers between his.

He instantly encased her hand with both of his, gripping them like a drowning man. 'I love you, Hayley. You make me a better person and I'm begging you for a second chance.'

A picture of a future with Tom beamed in her mind, but she stalled it. 'Tom, I never want to relive this last week. Sighted or unsighted, no one can totally protect me, just like I can't totally protect you. How do I know that you're not going to retreat on me again?'

'Because I *never* want to relive this last week again either and should I ever fall back on old habits, you'll remind me of how miserable I was without you and how much I need you.' He brought one hand up to cup her cheek. 'You've taught me more than you'll ever know, but most importantly you've opened my eyes and shown me that my life with you is stronger, richer and happier. I can only hope that you believe your life with me is stronger, richer and happier too.'

His heartfelt words all but demolished her doubts and she put her finger under his chin, tilting his head slightly so she could look directly into his eyes. She saw a deep and abiding love, and a pledge of commitment to her. He spoke the absolute truth. He really did love her. Warmth spread through her, clearing away the remnants of her misgivings, and the axis of her world righted itself, spinning on joy.

She touched his cheek. 'I found a peace with you I've never known. I love you, Tom Jordan.'

Relief flooded his handsome face and he pulled her close, his lips seeking hers. She met them with her own, welcoming the heat of his desire, and at the same time recognising the change in it. This time love underpinned his need and it flowed through her as a living thing, touching every organ, bone, muscle, tendon, tissue and cell until she almost cried out from the intensity of it.

When he finally broke the kiss he said, 'You love me and I'm the luckiest man alive.'

She leaned into him, still not quite believing that he'd come back and found her. 'Don't ever forget it,' she half teased.

'I won't. I promise.' He stroked her hair. 'Hayley?'

Her senses reeled with the musky smell of him, the solid feel of him in her arms, and she never wanted to move. 'Mmm.'

'I spoke to Richard Hewitson today.'

She raised her head to look at him, holding her breath before she finally spoke. 'And?'

He grinned. 'I'm the new associate professor at Parkes School of Medicine, and as well as lecturing I'm setting up a support structure for disadvantaged students. Not only for those enrolled in the programme but for students who aren't here yet, like Jared. I'm going to help create pathways into medicine and then support the students when they're here, like Mick and Carol did for me.'

He's found his way. Happiness flooded her and she kissed his cheek. 'That's fantastic, Tom. I've always said you had great rapport with young people.'

His mouth kicked up at one corner. 'And I finally heard you.' He pressed a kiss into her hair. 'You know, not being able to operate will always feel like I've lost a limb, but there's nothing I can do to get my sight back. I have to move on, and being blind has led me to this new job and the possibility of helping kids just like me. I know it's going to challenge me in new and different ways, and that feels exciting. Most importantly, my blindness led me to you.'

His love and sincerity cocooned her and she rested her forehead against his. 'If I've opened your eyes then you've given me back the dark. Thank you.'

His hand curved around the back of her neck. 'Like you told me, we make a good team. Will you make us a permanent team by marrying me?'

She didn't even try to stifle her squeal of delight as she enthusiastically threw her arms around his neck. 'Yes. Oh, yes.'

He swayed from her body slam and grinned at her. 'I love your answer, but do you have a couch we could sit on before you knock me off my feet?'

'No.' She dropped her voice to the smoky timbre she knew he adored. 'But I do have a bed.'

His eyes flared with love and desire. 'Even better.'

'I'm full of good ideas.' She took his hand. 'Follow me.'

His fingers closed around hers. 'I'll follow you anywhere, Hayley.'

Her heart melted with happiness. 'And I'll walk beside you for the rest of my life.'

Smiling, he brought her hand to his mouth and kissed it, and she knew she was home.

EPILOGUE

Tom Jordan—Prof to almost everyone—felt his academic robes slide over his knees as he rose to his feet and joined in the applause for the graduating class. Sixty new doctors would be commencing their internships in hospitals across Australia and Jared was one of them. Tom could only remember a couple of other times in his life that he'd felt this proud.

Hayley's hand slipped into his and he thought he heard her sniff. 'I can't believe he's going to be working at The Harbour.'

'Daddy, why is Jared throwing his funny hat in the air?'

He looked down at the daughter he'd never seen, but his picture of her was crystal clear in his mind. He'd held her within seconds of her birth, counted her fingers and toes, felt her snub nose, tangled his fingers in her masses of hair and had recognised the differences in her cries ahead of Hayley. 'He's celebrating, Sasha. This is his special day.'

'Like my party?' Sasha had recently turned five and her voice sounded hopeful. 'Is there cake?'

His hand ruffled her silky hair. 'Yes, Nanna Carol made Jared a great big cake.'

'When Mummy was at the hospital?'

'That's right.' Hayley was now a consultant at The Harbour and had two registrars working under her.

People started moving around him and Hayley said, 'We should probably go now so we're home before our guests arrive. Sasha, hold my hand, please.'

Tom reached down, his left hand clasping leather. 'Forward, Baxter.'

His guide dog rose and safely guided him through the crowd, the way he'd been doing for seven years, and it constantly amazed Tom how expert he was at it. He smiled when he thought back to when he and Hayley had got married and how hard she'd worked to convince him that a guide dog would suit him perfectly. Years on, he knew that Hayley understood him almost better than he understood himself, and as a result he was much more open to her suggestions. He loved having a dog and couldn't imagine himself without one.

Two hours later, the party was in full swing. Tom had made a speech and was taking a breather from all the noise out on the balcony.

'Hey, Prof.'

Tom turned toward the voice. 'Hey, Dr Jared Perkins.'

Jared came and stood next to him. 'I've imagined being called "Doctor" for so long, but now it's here it sounds so weird. Six long years and I'm a doctor.'

Tom smiled. 'If you want to do neurosurgery, you're preparing to scale another mountain. Seven to ten more years.'

'Yeah, but it will be worth it. Without neurosurgery and without you I wouldn't be here. Thanks, Tom.'

The emotion in his friend's voice stirred the well in Tom he no longer hid, and he found Jared's shoulder and gave it a squeeze. 'It goes both ways, mate.'

'What does?'

Hayley's perfume and quick steps had preceded her, and Tom dropped his arm from Jared's shoulder and extended it toward his wife. 'Thanks go both ways.'

'They do.' Her smile sounded clear in her voice. 'Now you're dealing with rosters, Jared, Sasha's going to miss your Friday night visits. No other babysitter lets her get away with pizza in front of her favourite DVD.'

'Forget Sasha, we're going to miss our date night,' Tom teased. 'I wonder if there's another student in the Pathways Programme who might be interested in paid babysitting.'

'Jared!' Sasha's running feet hit the tiles of the balcony. 'Can you cut your cake, please?' She managed to elongate the 'please' with endearing charm.

Jared laughed. 'For you, Sash, anything.'

'Daddy, I can cut some cake for you.'

'Thank you, darling, but let Jared help you. Mummy and I will be there in a minute.'

When he heard the sound of their retreating feet ebb into the carpet, he pulled Hayley in close and a rush of tenderness made him smile. 'I just felt the baby bump.'

Hayley's hands slipped around his neck and she kissed him. 'In four months our life is going to change.'

He stroked her cheek. 'Life's always changing. We're going to have a new baby and a new puppy.'

'Poor Baxter. His retirement's going to be noisy and busy with a baby human and a puppy in the house. Sasha can't wait to play with him and I think she plans to dress him up for her tea parties.'

Tom still pinched himself every day that he'd been so blessed in his life. Hayley had changed his world and then Sasha had arrived and added to it in more ways than he could count. Now he could hardly wait to welcome their second child.

Tom laughed. 'Poor Baxter indeed. I had to be the tea-party guest last Wednesday.'

Hayley giggled. 'The work of a father is never done.'

'And I wouldn't have it any other way.'

'I might have known you two would be out here ca-noodling,' Carol interrupted with a chuckle. 'Akim and his wife have just arrived and they've brought basboosa cake.'

'We'll be right there, Carol.' But he didn't move his feet.

Hayley sighed. 'We should go.'

'We should and we will.' With the fingers of both hands he traced Hayley's face and then he brought her lips to meet his. He savoured her taste and felt her love pouring through him, and then he gave her all his love in return.

* * * * *